Runaway Ralph

Runaway Ralph

Beverly Cleary

illustrated by Louis Darling

A Yearling Book

Published by
Dell Publishing
a division of
The Bantam Doubleday Dell Publishing Group, Inc.
666 Fifth Avenue
New York, New York 10103

Yearling ® TM 913705, Dell Publishing Co., Inc.

ISBN: 0-440-77519-8

Book Club Edition

Reprinted by arrangement with William Morrow and
Company, Inc.

Printed in the United States of America

August 1980

20   19   18   17   16   15   14

KRI

To Louis Darling
1916-1970

Contents

Runaway
Ralph

1
Ralph Hears a Distant Bugle

The small brown mouse named Ralph who was hiding under the grandfather clock did not have much longer to wait before he could ride his motorcycle. The clock had struck eight already, and then eight thirty.

Ralph was the only mouse in the Mountain View Inn, a run-down hotel in the foothills of the Sierra Nevada, who owned a motorcycle. It was a mouse-sized red motorcycle, a present from a boy named Keith who had been a guest in Room 215 over the Fourth of July weekend. Ralph was proud of his motorcycle, but his brothers and sisters said he was selfish.

"I am not," said Ralph. "Keith gave the motorcycle to me."

That evening, while Ralph waited under the clock and watched the television set across the lobby, a man and a woman followed by a medium-sized boy walked into the hotel. They had the rumpled look of people who had driven many miles that day. The boy was wearing jeans, cowboy boots, and a white T-shirt with the words *Happy Acres Camp* stenciled across the front.

Ralph observed the boy with interest. He was the right kind of boy, a boy sure to like peanut-butter-and-jelly sandwiches. Since the day Keith had left the hotel, Ralph had longed for crumbs of a peanut-butter-and-jelly sandwich.

A grating, grinding noise came from the works of the grandfather clock. Ralph clapped his paws over his ears. The clock grumbled and groaned and managed to strike the hour. Nine o'clock! The time almost had come. The stroke of nine was followed by the slow sad notes of music that lingered and died mysteriously in the distance every night at this time.

"Did you hear that?" the man asked the boy. "It was the bugle at camp playing taps."

So that's what that music is, thought Ralph, who had puzzled over those notes all summer.

When the boy did not answer, his mother said, "Come on, Garf, cheer up. You're going to have a lot of fun at camp."

"Maybe," answered Garf, "but I doubt it."

The father looked annoyed. "You won't have any fun if you take that attitude," he said, and went to the desk to inquire about a room with an extra cot for the night.

Ralph could not understand the boy's behavior. He had often heard other young guests wearing the same kind of white T-shirt speak of a place called camp, but unlike this boy they always sounded eager and excited about going there. Ralph did not know exactly what a camp was, but since medium-sized boys and girls went there, he thought it must be a place where people ate peanut-butter-and-jelly sandwiches.

The desk clerk summoned old Matt, the elderly bellboy and hotel handyman, to show the family to their room. As Matt picked up their suitcases and led the way to the elevator, he said to Garf, "Well, young fellow, what are you going to have for breakfast tomorrow? Apple pie or chocolate cake?" Matt, who was not always popular with parents, was always liked by children.

The boy smiled faintly at Matt's joke as he followed the old man into the elevator. What that boy needs is a peanut-butter-and-jelly sandwich, thought Ralph.

When Matt returned to the lobby, Ralph watched him go out onto the hotel porch where he stood for a few minutes among the empty rocking chairs for his nightly look at the stars before he retired for the night. The night clerk, a college student hired for the summer, came on duty and settled down on a couch to read a thick book. Ralph's time almost had come. Sure enough, the clerk read a few pages, and then lay down on the couch with the book facedown on his chest and closed his eyes.

Ralph was free for the night! He darted under the television set where he had hidden his motorcycle and the crash helmet that Keith had made from half a pingpong ball lined with thistledown. He already had polished the chrome on his motorcycle by licking his paws and rubbing them over the dull spots. Now he set his crash helmet on his head, snapped the rubber band under his chin to hold it in place, and taking care to keep his tail out of the spokes mounted his motorcycle. Next he inhaled deeply and exhaling with a *Pb-pb-b-b-b* sound, the only sound that will make a miniature motorcycle go, sped out from under the television set and across the carpet.

Pb-pb-b-b-b! Ralph rode across the lobby

and into the hall. Up and down the hall
zoomed Ralph, and the joy of speed made up
for the long hours of hiding in dusty corners
waiting for night to come.

Up and down the hall rode Ralph until he
was too tired to take another big breath. Then
he parked his motorcycle in a shadowy corner,
hung his crash helmet on the handlebars, and
flattening himself slipped under a door into his
favorite room in the Inn. It was a stuffy room,
never very light even in daytime, and locked

when the last person left it at night. It was furnished with small tables and a row of high stools. The room was Ralph's favorite because he always could find peanuts on the floor, sometimes popcorn, and once in a great while a stuffed olive. Tonight he gobbled his fill of peanuts, wishing he had a little grape jelly to go with them, and managed, in spite of being somewhat fatter than when he had entered, to squeeze out again.

Pb-pb-b-b-b. Daredevil Ralph rode perilously close to the dangling hand of the night clerk sleeping on the couch before he tore the length of the hall. Ralph was exhilarated by speed, danger, and his own daring. *Pb-pb-b-b-b!* Back to the lobby!

As Ralph paused to take another deep breath his sharp ears caught the approaching squeaks of his little brothers and sisters and cousins, who rarely ventured into the lobby because they were afraid of the stuffed deer heads on the walls and the stuffed owl on the mantelpiece of the stone fireplace. "Drat!"

swore Ralph softly to himself. Ralph was in the process of taking a deep breath, so he could make a fast getaway, when his mother and Uncle Lester scurried from under a chair in front of him. Ralph's deep breath came out in a *poof*, and his motorcycle stopped.

"Ralph," said Uncle Lester, "it is time we had a talk."

Ralph did not answer. He did not want to talk. Neither did he want to listen, but he knew that he could not avoid his uncle's lecture. He only hoped it would end before the little mice managed to get down the stairs.

"You can't go on living like this," said Uncle Lester, "running around the lobby, watching television all day, and tearing around on that motorcycle all night."

"Yes," agreed Ralph's mother, a most fearful mouse whose whiskers trembled constantly with fright. She was afraid of people, vacuum cleaners, owls, cats, traps, and poisoned grain. She quivered at the slightest sound.

Ralph stared at the carpet.

"Look at you," said Uncle Lester. "Lint all over your whiskers."

Ralph brushed at his whiskers with one paw.

"And you're getting fat from eating peanuts you pick up in that—that *place*," continued Uncle Lester. "A bar is no place for a young mouse."

"You will fall in with evil companions," said his mother. "They will lead you into trouble."

"Nobody can lead me any place," said Ralph, "because I can go faster on my bike."

By now the little brothers and sisters and cousins had gathered to listen, wide-eyed with interest and pleasure.

One cousin, braver than the rest, said, "He thinks he's big, calling a motorcycle a bike."

"Ralph, you are sure to break your neck if you keep on riding that thing," said his mother.

"You *said* I could ride it," said Ralph sullenly. "You said I could if I wore my crash helmet and kept both paws on the handle grips."

"I know," admitted his mother with a sigh. "I can't imagine what I was thinking of."

The grandfather clock began to grind and groan. All of Ralph's family was alert, and when the clock began to strike they disappeared under chairs and behind draperies—all except Uncle Lester, and even he looked nervous.

"This is no life for a growing mouse," said Uncle Lester. "It is time you moved back upstairs to the mouse nest and helped lay in supplies for the lean months between summer and the ski season. You know nobody comes to this old hotel to spill crumbs as long as there is a vacant room in one of the new motels out on the highway."

The clock finished striking midnight, and Ralph's relatives crept out of their hiding places.

"He won't," said one of the bigger little cousins. "He won't because he's selfish."

"You keep out of this," said Ralph.

"He is! He is! He's just plain selfish!" squeaked the little brothers and sisters and cousins.

The night clerk stirred in his sleep, and all

the mice froze into silence until the sound of snores came from the couch. All hotel mice know they are safe from people who are snoring. The argument continued.

"He keeps everything for himself," complained a little brother.

"That's right," agreed another. "He never gives any of us a ride on his motorcycle."

"Now Ralph," said his mother, "it wouldn't hurt you to give the little mice a ride once in a while."

"I thought you said motorcycle riding was dangerous," Ralph reminded his mother.

"That's no way to talk to your mother," said Uncle Lester. "You don't have to speed. You can push your young relatives up and down the hall."

"Push them!" squeaked Ralph in horror. *Push* little mice up and down the hall on his beautiful motorcycle with its plastic seat and its pair of shining chromium mufflers! What a shocking idea. A motorcycle was not a kiddy car.

"Now Ralph, sharing your motorcycle won't

hurt you one bit," said his mother. "Don't look so sulky."

"Me first! Me first!" shrilled the little mice, pushing and shoving.

"Ralph, get that look off your face!"

Uncle Lester looked so stern that Ralph knew there was no way out. "Even the girls?" he asked.

"Of course," said his mother. "Quiet, children, or you will wake up the night clerk."

Ralph wished the little mice would wake up the night clerk, so he would have an excuse for hiding his motorcycle. However, his young relatives, who were, in Ralph's opinion, a fearful bunch, were silenced, and there was nothing for Ralph to do but boost the nearest little one up onto the seat of the motorcycle. "Gimme the crash helmet," demanded the passenger.

"What are you waiting for?" asked Uncle Lester. "Let him wear it."

Ralph removed his treasured helmet, placed it on the head of his small passenger, and

wheeled the awed little mouse down the hall and back. "More! More!" demanded the passenger.

"You had your turn." Ralph spoke shortly as he looked with distaste at his young relatives scrambling all over one another in their eagerness to be next. There were so many of them. Pushing them up and down the hall would take him all night. "Come on," he said crossly to his nearest cousin, as he clapped the crash helmet on his head and boosted him onto the plastic seat. "Let's get it over with."

"Faster!" demanded the cousin. "I want to go faster."

"You be quiet!" said Ralph. "You wanted a ride, and you're getting it."

Ralph soon found that pushing the motor-cycle along the bare floor at the edge of the hall was easier than pushing it through the carpet. Up and down the hall he trudged with one little mouse after another, while he longed to be riding off into the kitchen where the lino-leum made the best speedway in the hotel.

Up and down the hall plodded Ralph with brothers, sisters, cousins. He grew more and more rebellious as the stars outside the hotel grew dim above the pine trees. The motorcycle was his. It was given to him by a boy to ride, not to use as a kiddy car for a lot of wiggly, squirmy little mice. A motorcycle was not a toy. Why couldn't his mother and Uncle Lester understand? Because they were too old to understand. Too old and too timid, that was why.

Ralph felt sorry for himself, caught as he was between two generations of mice. (Most of his own litter had died from eating poisoned grain put out by a particularly disagreeable cook.) There was the older generation of mice, who worried about safety and being able to scrounge enough crumbs to tide them over the lean months between the summer season and the ski season. Then there was the younger generation of silly little mice, who were always busy wiggling, climbing all over one another, and gobbling up crumbs as fast as they were brought to the mouse nest. Nobody understood Ralph, which was his whole trouble.

Night was fading and the chirp of a bird out in the pines told Ralph that the hotel was about to come to life. The night clerk soon would awaken and close his book, and the cook soon would be rattling pans in the kitchen.

A cousin, braver than most, came running down the hall where Ralph was wearily pushing the motorcycle. "You aren't fair," he scolded. "You've given him three rides and some of the others two and me only one."

Ralph stopped in his tracks. "Do you mean to stand there and tell me some of you have had more than one ride?"

"Yes," was the answer. "And I'm going to

tell Uncle Lester on you. Then you'll really catch it."

Ralph was too angry to squeak. He snatched his helmet from the head of his passenger, tipped him off onto the floor, and mounted his motorcycle while taking a deep breath. *Pb-pb-b-b-b*. Ralph shot down the hall into the lobby.

The first pale rays of morning sun filtered through the pines, which now were filled with joyously chirping birds. The night clerk stirred. All the little mice looked frightened and scuttled toward the stairs and the safety of their nests of shredded Kleenex. The night clerk sat up, yawned, stretched and scratched his chest, giving Ralph just enough time to garage his motorcycle in the dark corner under the television set before the last shadow of night faded from the old hotel.

Ready to rest and filled with bitter thoughts, Ralph set his crash helmet on the dusty carpet and sat down with his back resting against the front wheel of his motorcycle. The grown-up mice should not make him use his beautiful motorcycle as a toy to amuse a lot of squirmy, ungrateful little relatives, who were growing up and soon would insist on riding by themselves. And Uncle Lester would insist that Ralph let them. Well, he wouldn't. Never again would he use the motorcycle as a toy. He did not care what Uncle Lester or anyone said.

Ralph did not want to grow up to be a crumb-scrounging mouse like Uncle Lester. He did not want to settle down in a nest of shredded Kleenex behind the baseboard of the linen room. He wanted a life of speed and danger and excitement. He wanted to be free —free to do as he pleased and go when he pleased on his shiny red motorcycle.

The clock struck six, and in the distance Ralph heard the notes of the distant bugle, this time lively notes that seemed a summons to excitement and adventure and, now that he knew where the notes came from, peanut-butter-and-jelly sandwiches. Before the notes had died away, Ralph heard the laughter and shouts of medium-sized boys and girls who must be about the age of Keith, the boy who had understood mice and who had given Ralph the motorcycle.

The rousing notes of the bugle and the laughter and shouting increased the feeling of rebellion within Ralph. As the last strains of the bugle call hovered in the clear mountain air, Ralph made up his mind. He knew now what he was going to do. He was going to run away.

2

The Open Road

Too excited to hide under the grandfather clock where he could watch television, Ralph spent the day beside his motorcycle under the television set watching life in the lobby and waiting for night to come. Luggage was set down with a thump. Guests complained that there were not enough towels in their rooms, and when the guests had gone, the desk clerk said to Matt, "What do they think this is? The Waldorf?"

Ralph listened as the manager of the hotel spoke sharply to the housekeeper about the cigarette ashes on the carpet. The housekeeper spoke even more sharply to the maid, who ran the vacuum cleaner so carelessly that Ralph was not even frightened. He was too busy thinking of the night that lay ahead. When the boy called Garf clumped àcross the lobby in his new cowboy boots on his way to Happy Acres Camp, Ralph longed to follow him out the front door and down the steps.

Late in the afternoon new guests straggled into the hotel. Some looked at the shabby furniture and dusty deer heads and left. Others, too tired from driving to look further, stayed. When the television set was turned on, Ralph polished the chrome on his motorcycle with his paws. When the set was silent, he napped, too excited to sleep soundly. At last the bugle in the distance played its slow sad notes, and old Matt left the front door open as he went out on the porch to look at the stars.

The moment had come! Ralph snapped his

crash helmet in place. He grasped the handle-bars and pushed his motorcycle out from its hiding place, avoiding the attention of the night clerk by guiding it along the edge of the baseboard to the front door. On the porch he mounted and with a vigorous *Pb-pb-b-b-b* rode across the cracked concrete to Matt's feet at the top of the steps.

"Hi," said Ralph, who was able to talk to animals and to any human being who loved speed and motorcycles and who understood that the only way to make a miniature motor-cycle go was to make a sputtering noise that sounded like a big motorcycle.

"Why, hello there, young fellow," said Matt. "Just where do you think you're going?"

"I'm running away," said Ralph. "On my motorcycle."

"You don't say!" exclaimed Matt.

"Yes. I've had enough of this place," said Ralph. "I'm going someplace where I can be free."

"You want to get away from your family,"

said Matt, grasping the situation at once. "You want to be independent."

"That's right," said Ralph. "I'm tired of being bossed around by my mother and Uncle Lester. I'm fed up with my pesty little brothers and sisters and cousins. I don't want to grow up to be another crumb-scrounging mouse. I want adventure and excitement, and I'm going to ride off on my motorcycle and find it."

"Sounds good," observed Matt. "I wish I could do the same. Just ride off into the night on a motorcycle. I always wanted a motorcycle, but I never could afford one. When I was young I had to help my folks, and then I had a family of my own to take care of. Now that my family has grown up and gone away, I'm too old for a motorcycle."

The mouse and the man were silent a moment before Ralph said, "Well, I guess I'd better be going."

"So long," said Matt. "Good luck. I'm going to miss you. It always cheered me up to see you tearing around the halls like a little daredevil. Made the suitcases seem lighter somehow." With that parting comment he turned and started back toward the door of the hotel.

"Hey, wait!" squeaked Ralph.

Matt turned. "You want something?"

For some reason Ralph hesitated before he said, "I was wondering if you would lift my motorcycle down the steps for me."

"And I was wondering how you were going to manage," remarked Matt, but he did not move to help Ralph.

"Uh . . . I'd like to get started," said Ralph. "I have a long way to go tonight."

"Sorry, I can't help you out," said Matt.

Ralph was astounded. For a grown-up human being, Matt always had been cooperative. "How come?" he demanded.

"If I lifted your motorcycle down the steps, you would be depending on me," said Matt, "and depending on others is not being independent."

Ralph was bewildered. "But how am I going to get my motorcycle down the steps without breaking it?"

"I don't know," admitted Matt. "I just hope

I don't have to come out here in the morning and sweep up pieces of red motorcycle." He turned then and went back into the hotel, closing the door behind him.

"Well, how do you like that!" said Ralph to himself. "And all the time I thought he was my friend."

Off in the distance an owl hooted. The night suddenly seemed vast, and a mouse a very small creature indeed. The row of empty chairs rocking in the breeze made Ralph nervous. He could not get over the feeling there were unseen people sitting in them, ghosts who might at any moment chase him and steal his motorcycle. He looked down at the three concrete steps and the curve of the driveway below them. His motorcycle was a good sturdy vehicle, but it would never survive three bounces on concrete. It would be smashed to bits—bits for Matt to sweep up in the morning.

Suddenly Ralph was angry. He was furious at the way his old friend had treated him.

He would show Matt that he could manage without help. Matt would come out in the morning expecting to find Ralph waiting to be let in, but Ralph would fool him. He wouldn't be waiting, and there wouldn't be any broken motorcycle at the foot of the steps either.

Ralph set about finding a solution to his problem. He looked at the ghostly rocking chairs, the cracked concrete porch, the steps, and the asphalt driveway below. Once Ralph had taken the trouble to look, the solution to getting his motorcycle down the steps seemed surprisingly easy. About three inches below the porch on either side of the steps was a sloping section of concrete, a sort of ramp intended as an edge to the steps. The two ramps were about ten inches wide and each sloped down to a flat section. Below each flat section was a shrub that had been pruned into a somewhat lopsided ball of leaves.

All Ralph had to do was ride his motorcycle over the edge, down the slope and into the shrub, which would break his fall and let him slide gently through the leaves to the ground. The only problem was that terrifying three-inch drop from the porch to the slanting concrete, but Ralph was sure that with a cool head and steady paws he could manage. He would show old Matt a thing or two!

Ralph wheeled his motorcycle back from the edge of the porch, but in line with one of the concrete ramps. High speed would be best, he decided, speed fast enough to carry him over the edge without wobbling so that he would land on the ramp on both wheels. Ralph's heart was pounding as he mounted his motorcycle, but his head was cool and his paws steady on the handle grips.

Ralph drew a deep breath. *Pb-pb-b-b-b.* His paws tightened on the handle grips. He rode smoothly toward the edge of the porch. He held his breath as he shot out into space as he had planned. There was a sudden heart-shaking drop before the tires hit the ramp.

At this point everything went wrong. Be-

fore Ralph realized what was happening, the
motorcycle shot down the ramp, which was
worn smooth by the many children who had
slid down it. Ralph flew into the air and fell
upside down into the shrub. He lost his grip
on the motorcycle and felt himself brushed
by leaves and scratched by twigs until he

came to rest wedged into the crotch of a small branch. His helmet had fallen off, one ear was scratched, and he was badly frightened, but he was not injured.

When Ralph had caught his breath and his heart no longer pounded against his ribs, he boosted himself up so that he was sitting in the crotch of the twig. The shrub was not the leafy cushion he had expected. From his perch in the center he could see that the leaves grew only at the tips of the twigs and that the bush, which had looked soft and springy from the outside, was on the inside leafless and spiky with dead twigs.

My motorcycle, thought Ralph frantically. Where is it? Then he saw it, far above his head hanging on a twig by its back wheel. His helmet, however, had bounced to the ground.

Ralph did the only thing he could do and that was climb up to his motorcycle and start chewing. The twig that held the motorcycle had a dry and dusty taste, but Ralph chewed until it snapped and the motorcycle slid down to the crotch of the twig below. Ralph climbed down, and when he could not free the motorcycle with his paws, he started chewing once more. No little cousin was ever going to say to him, What happened to your motorcycle, Ralph? Huh? What happened to your motorcycle?

Ralph chewed his motorcycle from one twig to the next, and the lower he went, the thicker the twigs became. By the time the motorcycle finally dropped to the ground beside the helmet, Ralph's jaws ached. He dragged the motorcycle across the weedy patch of lawn to the driveway and was about to mount when the door of the hotel unexpectedly opened and old Matt, in pajamas and bathrobe, stepped out on the porch and looked around.

"The little fellow must have managed to get his motorcycle down the steps somehow," Ralph heard Matt mutter to himself. "Now maybe I can get to sleep."

I guess I showed you, thought Ralph grimly, as he mounted his motorcycle and sped off down the open road, off into the dark and

scary night. So long, brothers, sisters, cousins! So long Uncle Lester! So long Matt! Ralph was on his way!

Pb-pb-b-b-b. Ralph bounced along the uneven driveway to the mountain highway where he quickly discovered that one of the ribbons of concrete pressed smooth by passing tires made a good highway for a mouse. He then made an even more exciting discovery — gravity. With a good fast start he could coast downhill with amazing speed. The halls of the Mountain View Inn were never like this.

Ralph sped through a night that fulfilled his dreams of freedom. It was a night of danger and adventure. Once when Ralph was frightened by the headlights of an approaching car, he swerved to the side of the road where he and his motorcycle were caught in the backdraft of the passing car and tumbled about like old gum wrappers and tossed into the weeds. Afterward Ralph was alert when he heard a car approaching and got off the road and clung to a weed until the car roared past. He was exhilarated by this test of his skill. Toward dawn logging trucks began to rumble down the mountain, shaking the earth as they came. Ralph never had seen anything so terrifying as those great double-tired monsters with logs lashed to their truckbeds barreling down the center of the highway, and he knew the time had come to hide for the day. He ate some dusty weed seeds, drank dew, slept under a leaf, and started off once more at nightfall toward the sound of the bugle.

Between cars and trucks Ralph tore along down the highway through the shadows of the night. This ride was the freedom he had dreamed of—speed without effort. Once the thought crossed his mind that if he should ever want to return to the Mountain View Inn, he could never make it back up the mountain under his own power. What a silly thought! Why should he ever want to go back to the Inn when he could travel this way?

On the third night of Ralph's journey, as darkness faded and the pine trees gave way to scrub oak, Ralph found himself out in the open where there were no sheltering shadows. A milk truck rattled past on its way to the Mountain View Inn. Blackbirds greeted the dawn with bursts of gurgling song, and not far away a rooster crowed. A pheasant flew low across the road, startling Ralph and causing him to collide with a piece of gravel. The road, which now followed an irrigation

ditch, had leveled off and Ralph had to pro-
duce his own power.

Pb-pb-b-b-b. As Ralph putted along on his
motorcycle, daylight made him uneasy. He
was looking for a place to hide when the notes
of the bugle, so close he felt as if they might
shatter him, burst forth in the lively morning
tune. Before they died away, laughter and
shouts filled the air. Medium-sized boys
and girls! Peanut-butter-and-jelly sandwiches!
Ralph had reached his destination.

Ralph wished old Matt could see him as
he rode off the road and bounced onto a gravel
lane that crossed a small bridge over the irrigation ditch. Ahead lay a number of low,
weathered buildings surrounded by lawn and
shaded by walnut trees. Boys and girls were
washing their faces in washbasins set on
benches.

A big brown dog, barking furiously, came
bounding toward Ralph, who stopped, frozen
with terror. The dog stopped, too, so suddenly
he nearly sat down in the gravel. He recovered

himself and approached, snuffling with his wet black nose. Ralph sat with his paws clutching his handle grips in fear while the horrible black nose sniffed him.

"And just who do you think you are?" asked the dog.

"Quiet, Sam!" yelled a boy.

"A m-mouse." Ralph felt very, very meek.

Sam eyed Ralph with curiosity. "Where did you get the motorcycle?" he wanted to know.

"A boy gave it to me." Ralph was beginning to feel slightly braver, but only slightly. That big dog could gobble a mouse in one gulp. But not if I hang onto my motorcycle, thought Ralph, feeling that his courage had not deserted him entirely. A dog would not eat a motorcycle.

"No kidding," said Sam. "A mouse-sized motorcycle! Where did you come from?"

"The Mountain View Inn."

"That run-down place," said Sam. "I'm not surprised the mice are deserting it. Where are you going?"

"Well . . . here, I guess," said Ralph. "I followed the sound of the bugle. I wanted to be near medium-sized children and peanut-butter-and-jelly sandwiches."

"Sorry," said Sam. "You can't come in here. I'm the watchdog of Happy Acres Camp, and it's my job to protect the camp."

"Aw, come on," said Ralph, who was beginning to see that Sam was not really a ferocious dog. "I'm just a mouse."

Sam looked uncomfortable. Obviously he was a dog that liked to please everyone. "I would let you in if I could, but my orders are to keep out anyone who doesn't belong here."

Ralph hunched down on his motorcycle. "Please. I'm just a teeny little brown mouse. Nobody would even notice me."

Sam's honest brown face looked worried. "No," he said at last. "I can't let you in. I have my orders from Aunt Jill and Uncle Steve in the camp office. They are in charge here."

"I've had a long hard trip," said Ralph. "I'm tired and I'm hungry."

Sam looked so worried that Ralph pressed his advantage. "You know boys like mice. They would be glad to have me."

Sam looked back toward a white building under the walnut trees. Then he looked down at Ralph. "I tell you I can't do it," he said. "If I let you come in I'd be breaking my orders. I'm already in trouble because a car came along in the middle of the night and dumped a box of kittens. It got away before I could rouse anybody."

"Kittens!" squeaked Ralph in horror.

"I have the worst time with kittens," Sam's voice was gloomy. "People are always dumping kittens here, because they know girls will beg their parents to let them take them home."

"Very many kittens?" asked Ralph, who was feeling nervous once more.

"Too many," said Sam. "We already had three kittens that belonged here, and the other night six more were dumped. And once they are here, I'm not allowed to chase them. I tell you, it isn't fair. If there's one thing I can't stand, it's kittens. Silly little things with no sense of responsibility."

Sam's troubles made Ralph feel cocky once more. "If you're a watchdog, watch me!" he .said, and taking a deep breath he shot between Sam's legs and out the other side before the surprised dog could turn around. Ralph swerved around a green walnut lying on the ground and into a patch of weeds beside a nearby building.

"Come back here," barked Sam. "You aren't supposed to do that." He began to snuffle around in the weeds.

Ralph had not expected to be snuffled for. He had thought that once he was inside the camp, Sam would give up.

Sam growled and moved his nose around in the weeds like a doggy vacuum cleaner. Unable to ride, Ralph pushed his motorcycle farther back into the weeds. The wet black nose parted the stalks, but Ralph was saved by a gopher hole. He dragged his motorcycle into its shelter.

"Oh, no, you don't," growled Sam, and began to dig with his powerful front paws. Dirt began to fly. Pulling his motorcycle after him, Ralph waded farther back through the loose dirt into the gopher hole. Faster went the paws.

"Hey, everybody! Sam's after a gopher!" a

boy yelled, and Ralph could feel feet pounding on the ground overhead.

"Go get him, Sam!" urged another boy.

"Sickum, Sam," everyone seemed to be saying at once.

"You're being mean to the gopher," protested a girl.

Several girls' voices began to yell, "Go, gopher, go!"

Faster and faster flew the paws with their strong toenails. Sam was panting now. Ralph pushed farther and farther back into the gopher run until a disagreeable voice ahead of him said, "And where do you think you're going?"

"Eek!" squeaked Ralph, face to face with the owner of the gopher run. He hastily pushed his motorcycle, which he had been pulling, ahead of him for protection.

"Beat it," said the gopher, squinting at Ralph. "I didn't dig this tunnel for mice."

The digging paws were coming closer. "Attaboy, Sam!" shouted the boys.

"Go, gopher, go!" shouted the girls.

Even the gopher looked uneasy. "Please," pleaded Ralph, "save me from that beast."

The gopher was more interested in saving himself. Already he was beginning to move farther down the run. "You can stay until that dog stops digging and no longer," he said, and fled off into the network of tunnels.

Not far away a bell clanged. "Breakfast! Chow time!" yelled the boys, and the feet that went pounding off in the direction of the bell shook the ground overhead. The paws stopped churning, but overhead Ralph could hear the sound of panting. Sam poked his fearsome snout into the gopher hole for one last sniff before he too trotted off for breakfast.

"Whew!" gasped Ralph, leaning against his motorcycle. He had pictured camp as a place where boys would bring him peanut-butter-and-jelly sandwiches, not this dark and dusty tunnel inhabited by a grouchy gopher.

3
An
Educational
Toy

Ralph did not rest long.

"On your feet, mouse," said the gopher, appearing from the dark recesses of the gopher run. "You can go now."

"Do I have to?" pleaded Ralph, nervously eyeing the gopher's long curving teeth. "I've come a long way, and I need a day's sleep."

"Go on, beat it." The gopher stared at Ralph with his nearsighted eyes. "This is my run, and I don't want it cluttered up with mice."

"Please." Ralph tried to sound pitiful. "I'm just a little mouse, and I've had a long, hard trip."

"I know you mice," answered the gopher. "You are little and you look helpless, but when you move in you take over." Then he added in a more kindly tone, "Anyway, you had better get out while you can. That dog will eat his breakfast and go off on his round of inspection, and when he sees all the dirt he churned up, he'll start digging again."

"Maybe you're right," admitted Ralph, who was not eager to share a tunnel with a grouchy gopher. He pushed his motorcycle up toward the circle of light that was the entrance to the gopher run. There he paused until his eyes became accustomed to the sunlight.

A stray chicken wandered across the lawn under the walnut trees. A horse whinnied from the barn, and from the dining hall came the laughter and chatter of boys and girls and the clatter of silverware. The place seemed safe enough at the moment. Ralph permitted himself a leisurely but bumpy ride along a path that led to a small weathered building shaded by an arbor of grape vines. At the corner of the building he found a clump of bamboo, which offered the possibility of shelter. The fallen leaves and husks of the young bamboo shoots were broad and smooth, and the dried edges curled. He laid his motorcycle at the foot of the bamboo and pulled a husk over it. The edges curled around it so that it was hidden completely. He put his helmet under another husk, and too tired to scrounge for food Ralph crawled under a third husk.

Ah-h. Ralph curled himself into a cozy ball. The leaves beneath him were springy. The husk above him was smooth and silky and curled protectingly around him. Ralph had not been so comfortable for a long, long time. A delicious fragrance of hot cakes drifted from the dining hall, reminding Ralph of the dining room of the Mountain View Inn. The campers began to sing:

"The horses stand around,

> Their feet are on the ground.
> Oh, who will wind the clock,
> While I'm away, away."

Ralph wondered if Matt had wound the clock in the lobby. Perhaps Matt was searching for a broken motorcycle in the shrubbery at the foot of the steps of the Mountain View Inn. Well, he wouldn't find it! Now all Ralph wanted was a peanut-butter-and-jelly sandwich. . . . Ralph slept more soundly than he had ever slept before.

The next thing Ralph knew a weight was pressing him into the bamboo leaves. He squirmed, but the weight pressed harder. He heard a cat's voice say, "Now watch carefully. This is the way to handle a mouse."

That greeting opened Ralph's eyes in a hurry! He saw to his horror that he was pinned to the leaves by the paw of a coldhearted tomcat and was surrounded by a mother cat and a litter of wide-eyed kittens. Ralph simply closed his eyes again and tried to pretend

he was not there. He could not believe what
was happening. Cats were something that happened to other mice, not to Ralph. Now he
wished he had listened when his mother had
tried to warn him, as she so often did, about
cats, owls, people, traps, poisoned grain, and
vacuum cleaners.

"Children, pay attention," said the mother
cat to her kittens. "A live mouse is an interesting and instructive plaything."

Ralph felt quite miserable enough without
having to be educational as well.

"Now watch this," said the tomcat.

The weight was removed from Ralph's
body. A paw scooped him up and tossed him
into the air. Nothing like this ever had happened to Ralph before. He landed on his feet
and stood, frozen with terror, facing the cat.
He waited with every muscle tense for the cat
to pounce but nothing happened. The cat
who wore an interested expression on his horrible furry face, simply sat and watched.
Ralph was aware of the campers leaving the

dining hall and scattering to different parts of the camp, but he dared not look at them. If he watched his chance he might be able to make a run for it. The cat, apparently distracted by a butterfly, glanced away. Ralph leaped for freedom only to be brought to earth by a paw.

"That's the way to do it," said the tomcat. "Mice are stupid creatures who are easily fooled."

Ralph lay limp and still, the cat's evil claws curling around his body. If Ralph moved even a hairsbreadth, he would be stabbed in five places. Maybe if I play dead they will go away, he thought. Children walked in and out of the screen door nearby, but no one came to the rescue of the small, brown mouse behind the bamboo.

"He's trying to play dead," explained the tomcat, "but I can feel his heart beating beneath my paw."

Unfortunately, there was nothing Ralph could do about his heartbeat. If he ever got away from this cat, he would be a better

mouse. He would listen when his mother warned him about cats, owls, people, traps, poisoned grain, and vacuum cleaners. He would set a good example for his little brothers and sisters and cousins.

"Children forget that butterfly and watch closely," instructed the mother cat.

"This is the scoop-and-toss play," explained the tomcat, and the next thing Ralph knew he had been scooped up by the cat's paw and tossed into the air. He managed to land on all fours in the bamboo leaves, but he was too terrified of that clawed paw to move. The attention of the kittens, he was pleased to see, had wandered. One rolled over and tried to catch his tail. Another scampered off after a leaf. A third trotted after a girl who picked him up and carried him away. The tomcat appeared to lose interest in Ralph and sat calmly, his tail curved around his feet, looking up at the leaves fluttering on the bamboo stalks.

He thinks he's got me fooled, thought Ralph. If he moved, the cat was sure to pounce. If he did not move, the cat would pounce anyway. There was no way Ralph could win. He was doomed—doomed to be a mid-morning snack for a cat.

Luckily, Ralph did not have to make a decision. There was a sudden whacking noise on the fallen leaves and a cloud of something light and soft settled over him. Then he found himself being tumbled about as he was lifted from the ground.

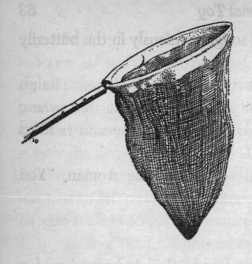

"Good for you, Garf," said a woman's voice. "What kind of butterfly did you catch?"

"It isn't a butterfly," answered the boy. "It's a mouse. I rescued him from Catso."

By now Ralph had managed to get his feet down and his head up and could see that he was suspended in the air in some sort of net. Through the mesh he could see a plump, cheerful woman, who was wearing slacks and a blouse. He also could see the boy, the same boy who had clumped through the Mountain View Inn in new cowboy boots, who was now holding him so ignominiously in the butterfly net.

Better a net than a paw, thought Ralph philosophically, because he felt that where there was a boy, there was hope. Boys liked mice.

"A mouse!" exclaimed the woman. "You caught a mouse in a butterfly net?"

"Yes," answered the boy, "and I'm going to keep him."

Where? wondered Ralph. In his pocket? He hoped so. A boy's pocket was apt to be warm and dark and full of crumbs. The cat, cheated of his prey, stalked off with his tail in the air trying to pretend in a most dignified manner that he did not want a mouse anyway.

"Good," said the woman enthusiastically, surprising Ralph. All the women he had known—the housekeeper, maids and guests of the hotel—referred to mice as nasty creatures or pesky rodents, and from Ralph's point of view spent their time trying to outwit perfectly harmless little animals. "We can find a place for him in our nature corner," suggested the woman, who Ralph decided must be the Aunt Jill Sam had mentioned. "Come on into the craft shop. I'm sure we have an old cage somewhere."

Ralph was disappointed. He had looked forward to a dark and crumby pocket. At the same time he was anxious. If he was to be trapped in a cage, how could he get back to his motorcycle?

The screen door creaked as it was opened, and Ralph found himself looking through the net at a room with long worktables and walls lined with shelves full of boxes, jars, and odds and ends. Seated on a bench were three girls, who were busy braiding with long thin strips of colored plastic. They appeared to ignore the boy until the woman rummaged around on the shelves and produced a small wire cage with an exercise wheel inside and a bottle for water fastened at one end. Suddenly the girls were interested.

"What's the cage for, Aunt Jill?" asked one

of them, as all three jumped up from the bench.

"Garf caught a mouse in his butterfly net," explained Aunt Jill. "He wants to keep it."

"In a butterfly net!" The girls found this feat funny. "Let me see! Let me see!" they begged.

Ralph found himself being poked out of the net and into the cage. The door was closed behind him and fastened. He scurried behind the exercise wheel where he sat trembling, partly from fright and partly from relief at being safe from the cat.

"Isn't he a darling?" cried the girls, their faces large and close to the cage bars. "Isn't he *sweet?* Those teeny-tiny ears. Look at those itsy-bitsy paws!"

Ralph looked for help toward the boy, who had stepped aside and now stood scowling beside the screen door.

"Aunt Jill, can we feed the mouse?" begged the girls. "Please, let us feed him."

Ralph turned his back and curled up into the smallest possible ball.

"The mouse belongs to Garfield," said Aunt Jill. "He gets to feed his own mouse."

"Skip it."

Ralph thought Garf sounded angry. He heard the boy's footsteps leave the craft shop and the screen door screech and slam as it opened and closed.

"What's the matter with him?" asked one of the girls, who sounded as if she did not really care.

"Girls, do you know what I think we should do?" asked Aunt Jill. "I think we should all help Garfield enjoy camp. This is his first time away from home, and he doesn't know anyone here. I think he's lonely."

"But he's *mean*," protested the girl with the sunburned nose. "He just stays off by himself."

"There's nothing mean about that," Aunt Jill pointed out.

"I know . . ." admitted the girl. "But he . . . oh, I don't know. Anyway, Garf is a funny name."

"Maybe he doesn't think so," said Aunt Jill.

Ralph could feel one of the girls trying to poke her finger through the bars of his cage. "At meals he won't talk or sing," she said, jabbing Ralph with a stick. "He just eats and then he gets up and walks out."

Ralph tried to draw himself into a tighter ball.

"See, he's outside just standing there," said another girl. "He practically never talks to anybody."

Aunt Jill lifted Ralph's cage up onto a shelf in the corner near a window. "Catching a mouse in a butterfly net is certainly doing something," she remarked. "I think Garf should take care of the mouse."

Ralph made up his mind not to budge. If he stayed perfectly still, sooner or later they would all go away and let him enjoy peace and quiet in his nice safe cage. Then maybe Garf would come back. He might even think of bringing a corner of a peanut-butter-and-jelly sandwich. Then Ralph would simply explain to Garf that he needed to get out of the cage.

because he had to take care of his motorcycle. He was quite sure that Garf could understand, for he looked like the kind of boy who was interested in speed and motorcycles and who would know how to make a miniature motorcycle go.

4

Chum

When Ralph awoke, the camp was dark. Crickets chirped in the weeds outside the craft shop. In the distance frogs croaked, were suddenly silent, and croaked again. Timidly Ralph began to investigate his new home. Someone had supplied him with food and water. A piece of paper had been dropped thoughtfully into one corner. Knowing that he was safe from the cat, Ralph nibbled at some dried corn and a lettuce leaf until his stomach was full. Then he shredded the paper, which was somewhat harder to chew than the Kleenex he had enjoyed at the Mountain View Inn, and spread it around his cage before he summoned enough courage to explore his exercise wheel.

Ralph climbed cautiously onto the wheel, which swung back and forth so alarmingly that he jumped off. He ran around his cage examining the wheel from every angle. Deciding that the worst that could happen to him was falling off, Ralph tried again. This time he stayed on the wheel, and when he became accustomed to the swinging motion, he tried a few cautious steps. The wheel spun pleasantly beneath his feet.

Ralph ran faster. The wheel increased its speed. Ralph raced as hard as he could run, and then stopped. To his astonishment, the wheel continued to spin, and Ralph was carried completely around the circle so that for an instant, before he began his descent, he was upside down at the top of the wheel. This ride was fun! When Ralph had coasted to a stop, he began to run again so that he could spin around the full circle once more. Round and round went Ralph as the shadows in the craft shop faded. Spinning on a wheel was as dangerous and as exciting as riding a motorcycle.

His motorcycle! Ralph leaped from the wheel to the side of the cage nearest the window. The rays of the rising sun slanted through the bamboo, but no matter how hard Ralph strained his eyes he could not catch even a glimpse of chrome or red metal. If only he had some way of knowing his motorcycle was still hidden beneath the bamboo husk.

An alarm clock went off in a lodge nearby, and a boy in rumpled pajamas stumbled out to blow the rousing bugle notes that brought the camp to life. Ralph busied himself scattering his shredded paper about his cage, nibbling his food, and racing on his wheel. While the campers were in the dining hall eating breakfast, Garf slipped into the craft shop, checked

on Ralph's food and water, and slipped out
again so quickly that Ralph only had begun to
summon his courage to speak. That's funny,
Ralph thought. The boy acts as if he's doing
something wrong.

After breakfast Aunt Jill and several boys
and girls straggled into the craft shop and settled down to make pictures by gluing dried
rice, peas, beans, and corn to scraps of ply-
wood. Mosaics, they called them. Such a waste
of good food, thought Ralph, recalling some of
the hard times he had gone through with his
family back at the Mountain View Inn. Those
campers were ruining enough food to keep a
mouse family healthy for weeks.

Before long the mosaic makers discovered
Ralph, who obliged them by racing on his
wheel.

"Hey, look at him loop the loop!" said a boy
named Pete.

"Isn't he darling!" cried a girl. Apparently
all girls called mice, at least mice in cages,
darling.

Ralph could not resist showing off by looping the loop once more, and when many hands pushed bits of the mosaics into his cage, he nibbled greedily. At least there was no scrounging at Happy Acres Camp.

The next time Garf slipped into the craft shop while everyone else was in the dining hall, Ralph gathered his courage to speak. "Say—" he began in a timid voice, but the boy must not have heard, because at that moment he began to sing uncertainly to himself:

> "Little Rabbit Fru-fru
> Hopping through the forest
> Scooping up the field mice
> And *banging* them on the head."

Ralph was stunned by the words Garf sang. What kind of boy would sing such a wicked song? Certainly not a boy a mouse could trust. Frightened and disappointed, he scuttled to the farthest corner of his cage and turned his back.

"Down came the Good Fairy and she said,
'Little Rabbit Fru-fru, I don't want you
Hopping through the forest
Scooping up the field mice
And *banging* them on the head.' "

As Ralph sat trembling in his corner he listened and was puzzled. Garf, with obvious pleasure, was singing the same words the campers were singing in the dining hall, but the tune was different. When their voices went up, Garf's went down. When their voices went down, Garf's went up. Sometimes his voice did neither, but wavered someplace in the middle.

Ralph was bitterly disappointed by the whole turn of events. Garf was not interested in speed and motorcycles. He was interested in singing and in banging field mice on the head.

The hot summer days droned on. Ralph was supplied with more food than he could possibly eat, and his exercise wheel kept him in trim. Whenever Catso sneaked into the craft shop and showed an interest in Ralph's cage, someone snatched him and shoved him out the door.

Life was safe, comfortable, and not unpleasant. From his cage near the window, Ralph had a good view of the camp. To the left through the bamboo he could see the boys' lodges. To the right were the girls' lodges. Before him lay the dining hall, the camp office, a trampoline, a swimming pool, and a circle of benches and old school desks in front of a platform that held a piano. Off to the right beyond the shade of the walnut trees, a pasture shimmered in the summer heat. Counselors, who were college students like the summer help at the Mountain View Inn, led the activities of the campers, and one counselor lived in each lodge with eight or ten campers.

Ralph always found something interesting to watch—campers spreading their sleeping bags out in the sun to air, counselors leading singing and directing skits around the campfire in the evening, boys racing to be first in

line when the bell was rung to announce
meals, boys and girls in cowboy boots or English riding boots going off toward the barn for
riding lessons.

Boys and girls played and kittens romped
under the walnut trees. Catso discovered a
small hole in the craft shop's rusty screen door,
which he explored with a paw as if it were a
mousehole, but faithful old Sam always arrived to tell him to move on.

Never once did Garf forget to care for
Ralph, and when he was not singing in his
strange voice, he sometimes spoke. "Hi, little
fellow," he would say, as he quickly detached
the water bottle from the cage and refilled it
at the sink. He even offered Ralph a sunflower
seed with his fingers.

Ralph was so lonely he was tempted to accept the seed for the sake of companionship.
Then he remembered the song about mice
getting banged on the head and retreated to
the corner of his cage.

One afternoon, when Ralph was particularly lonely, he decided that a boy who fed a mouse three times a day could not be so bad after all, and that the next time a sunflower seed was offered, he would venture out and accept it from the boy's fingers.

However, when Garf finally came, he began to sing again. This time the song was different from the one the campers were singing over in the dining hall. It provoked Ralph's curiosity, because he had heard others sing it, but had been unable to catch the words. The campers never sang this song when Aunt Jill was around, which made Ralph even more curious about the words. He was under the impression that they were not fit for grown-up ears, which of course made the song all the more interesting.

Garf sang and Ralph listened.

"Great green gobs of greasy grimy gopher
    guts,
Stimulated monkey feet,
Chopped-up baby parakeet—"

That was enough for Ralph! In his haste to hide he bumped into the spout of his water bottle and flooded one side of his cage. He found refuge behind a lettuce leaf, where he sat trembling with nerves and fright while he refused to listen to another word of that fearsome song. Why, the next line might be about mice! Ralph stayed hidden behind the leaf for a long, long time. He was now certain that there was no hope of ever communicating with Garf. Chopped-up baby parakeet! Garf actually relished the dreadful words.

Then one day not long after Ralph had concluded that he was doomed to loneliness, a freckle-faced girl wearing a baggy sweatshirt, shorts, and cowboy boots came into the craft shop carrying a cage at least ten times the size of Ralph's cage. She set it on the table in the nature corner. "Hi, Aunt Jill. I'm back, and here's Chum again," she announced. "I brought his box of food and bag of cedar shavings."

Aunt Jill dropped the strands of the lanyard she was demonstrating to hug the girl. "Well, hi, Lana! Welcome back! It's good to see you again. Chum will have a friend this year. A mouse one of the new boys caught in a butter-fly net." She lifted the big cage onto the shelf beside Ralph's cage.

Ralph sat on his wheel to get a better look at the new occupant of the nature corner, a cranky-looking animal with tan and white fur. Ralph, who had never seen such an animal, watched silently while the creature, whatever it was, shoved and pushed and stomped at the cedar shavings in his cage. He seemed to have difficulty arranging them to his satisfaction. Next he went through his food dish, picked out

a number of small green pellets, and shoved them outside his cage. The cedar shavings still did not please him, so he went back to shoving, pushing, and stomping. From time to time he paused to gnaw noisily at the bars of his cage with his long curving teeth.

Finally, when the bell had rung and the campers had gone off for their noon meal, Ralph, in his eagerness for companionship, could no longer remain silent. "What are you anyway?" he asked. "Some kind of fancy gopher?"

The animal spat a green pellet out of his cage before he shot Ralph a withering look of scorn. "Fancy gopher, indeed!" he sniffed.

"Well . . ." Ralph faltered. "I didn't know. You can't blame me for asking."

"I am a hamster," said the animal. "A *golden* hamster. I am clean, odorless, and alert."

"You don't look gold to me," said Ralph. "You look tan and hairy."

At that response the hamster turned his back on the mouse.

Ralph nibbled a kernel of corn before he made up his mind to try again. "Pretty nice place we have here," he remarked. "Plenty of food and water. Interesting things to watch."

The hamster climbed on his exercise wheel and sat swinging to and fro while he stared at Ralph. When Chum remained silent, Ralph continued, "It's safe from the cat, too."

Chum appeared never to blink his eyes. "Maybe," he said.

Ralph's whiskers trembled. That one word spoken by the hamster hinted at evils unknown to Ralph. Here was an animal who was wise in the ways of the world. Well, go on, thought Ralph impatiently, tell me more. Chum was silent.

Finally Ralph was forced to say, "How come that girl brought you here to Happy Acres?"

"It's a long story," said Chum.

"I'm not in any hurry," said Ralph. "Go on."

Chum spat the hull of a sunflower seed into the bottom of his cage. "I was one of thirteen hamsters, six girls and seven boys, born in the back room of a pet store."

"Thirteen." Ralph was awed. "That's bigger than my litter. What was it like, living in a pet store?"

"We had a happy, carefree childhood there in the cage in the back room," Chum continued. "There was plenty of food and water and fresh cedar shavings in the bottom of the cage. We slept all day, all thirteen of us, in a warm and cozy heap. Then at night as we grew older we would play. Oh, the fun we had those nights in the pet shop." Chum paused, a faraway look in his eyes.

"Go on," urged Ralph.

"Where was I?" asked Chum. "Oh, yes— the frolics we had at night. And then . . . and then. . . ." Chum's voice shook with emotion.

Ralph waited quietly until the hamster was able to continue. "One day I was sound asleep in the corner of the cage. By then we had grown a lot, and I was on the bottom of the heap, but I didn't feel squashed. I felt safe and cozy there beneath my brothers and sisters, when suddenly—" Chum stopped, unable to go on.

"Don't stop now," pleaded Ralph. "What happened?"

"—a great human hand, a hand that smelled of dog—"

Ralph shuddered.

"—reached in and picked up several of my brothers and sisters. Let me tell you, that woke us all up in a hurry. We were terrified. We scrambled around, trying to hide behind our mother, under the wheel, in some cedar shavings, anyplace. I was slower than the rest, because, you see, I was cramped from being slept on by brothers and sisters, and so the hand, that terribly doggy hand, got me. It didn't matter. That hand got all us youngsters and turned us upside down in a most undignified fashion, and then we were put into two cages, boys in one and girls in another."

"What for?" asked Ralph.

"Don't rush me," said Chum, picking up a

sunflower seed in his paws and cracking it with his teeth. When he had eaten the kernels, he continued. "Let me tell you, it was a terrible shock. Shortly after, the doggy hand picked up our cage and loaded it into what is called a station wagon."

"I know." Ralph was eager to show off his knowledge. "I used to see them in the parking lot outside the hotel. They were always full of children and luggage and sometimes a dog or two."

Chum ignored the interruption. "We soon found ours was not the only cage to go into the station wagon. Our sisters were loaded in beside us along with a box of turtles, a cage of rather downhearted canaries, and two large cages, one containing puppies and the other some very silly kittens. Oh yes, and a cage of white mice."

"*White* mice," said Ralph scornfully. "Anybody, not just owls, could see white mice in the dark."

"Then the man with the doggy-smelling

hands climbed into the front seat along with his wife, and we were off."

"Where to?" asked Ralph.

"The county fair," answered Chum, "and it was a terrible trip. Kittens mewed, puppies whimpered, turtles scrabbled around in their box—"

"What's a county fair?" interrupted Ralph.

"A noisy place," said Chum. "It's full of people yelling, children laughing and shrieking, machinery that whirls and spins and plays music, all sorts of animals that neigh and moo and baa. It was hot and dusty, and our cages were set out in a booth. By that time we hamsters were exhausted. It had been light for several hours, and we hadn't had a wink of sleep."

"I know what you mean," said Ralph with feeling.

"That was only the beginning," continued Chum. "A steady stream of people, mostly children, passed our cages. Big, little, most of them sticky and all of them noisy. 'Look,

Mommy! Look, Daddy! Look at the darling little hamsters. I want one. Daddy, buy me a hamster!' All morning long. Parents were better. 'Don't be silly. Of course you can't have a hamster. You didn't take care of the last hamster you had. Come along. We don't have time to look at hamsters.' Then a whole busload of children, all of them wearing white T-shirts with letters across the front—"

"Camp T-shirts," interrupted Ralph knowledgeably. "From Happy Acres."

"—came crowding around the booth. They didn't have any parents with them so they bought pets."

"You?" asked Ralph.

"Me," said Chum. "I was bought by that grubby girl with freckles. To make a long story short, the doggy hand stuffed me into a hot little cardboard box with a few so-called air holes poked into it, and I spent the rest of the day being jounced around, peeked at, and fed bits of Karmel-Korn."

"Sounds good," said Ralph.

"Maybe to a mouse." There was a touch of scorn in Chum's voice. "We rode in a bus to this camp, where a counselor put together a makeshift cage out of a bucket with a piece of screen bent over the top. After a few days the girl's family arrived. There was quite a fuss when the parents saw that their daughter owned a hamster, but her two little brothers set up such a howl that once more I was stuffed into a box with so-called air holes, and after more bouncing and jouncing I arrived at the family's house where I was put into this cage where I have lived ever since. Poked at with pencils whenever the children's horrid little friends came over to play. Fed hamster food full of nasty little alfalfa pellets that I keep shoving out of my cage. You'd think they would catch on after a while, but no, they just keep on feeding me food mixed with alfalfa pellets. The worst part of my life is that I never get a full day's sleep. Someone's always moving the cage to dust, rattling something against the bars, running the vacuum cleaner, practicing violin lessons. It's not an easy life, let me tell you."

"But how did you get back to camp?" Ralph wanted to know.

"Last year when Lana was packing her duffle bag for camp, her mother said that since the people who ran the camp had let her buy me, they could put up with me for two weeks. *She* was tired of reminding Lana to feed me and clean my cage, and she wanted a vacation herself. She said the same thing this year. So here I am at camp for the third time. Oh well, at least it's a change, and nobody runs a vacuum cleaner or practices the violin near my cage."

Ralph was silent. Chum had given him a lot to think about. Like Chum he sat swinging to and fro on his wheel, swinging and thinking. And as he swung and thought, something caught his eye.

It was the striped forepaw of Catso reaching through the hole in the rusty screen door. Ralph watched in frightened fascination. The screen bulged from the pressure of Catso's

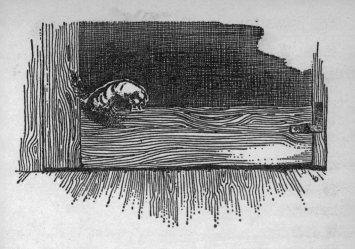

shoulder as the paw groped and searched. The rusted screen stretched, and the evil paw with its claw unsheathed reached farther into the craft shop.

Where's Sam? thought Ralph in terror. Why isn't that watchdog watching? The paw withdrew, and Catso's face pressed into the hole. His evil green eyes searched the craft shop. Ralph shrank into a ball in the farthest corner of his cage until he heard a short bark from Sam and summoned his courage to look around. Catso was gone, but the hole in the rusty screen remained.

5

The Personul Mowse

Ralph's life in the cage was never the same after the arrival of the hamster. Chum was picky about his food and fussy about his house-keeping. One corner of his cage had to be his bathroom, another his sleeping quarters, a third the storehouse for the food he liked. He was forever pushing, shoving, and stomping his cedar shavings. His exercise wheel rasped and creaked whenever he ran, usually while

Ralph was trying to nap. He had a particularly irritating way of gnawing noisily at the bars of his cage.

"Why do you do that?" asked Ralph. "You can't chew through metal."

"I'm not trying to chew through the bars," said Chum. "I'm wearing down my teeth."

Ralph was astounded. "Don't you want teeth?" he asked, thinking how dependent he was upon his own sharp teeth.

"If I don't chew something hard, my teeth will grow so long I won't be able to eat," Chum explained impatiently. "I chew the bars, because Lana is too stupid to give me anything hard to chew."

"Oh," said Ralph, grateful that his teeth did not continue to grow. Chum had another habit that disturbed Ralph. He nipped at Lana whenever she tried to pick him up.

"That's not nice," said Ralph one day, when he had seen Lana hastily withdraw her hand from her pet's cage. "That's biting the hand that feeds you."

"I have some rights," said Chum. "If I let Lana pick me up, I never would have any peace. Believe me, I know. I made the mistake of letting her pick me up just once, and when she tried to stuff me into a doll's sweater, I knew once was enough."

Chum also sat for long periods of time swinging gently on his wheel and staring with unblinking eyes at nothing at all.

"Why do you sit there like that?" asked Ralph, who liked to be busy when he was awake.

"I'm thinking," answered Chum.

"Thinking about what?" Ralph wanted to know.

"I am a philosopher," said Chum. "I think about life."

"Life?" Ralph was puzzled. "What do you mean?"

Chum sat staring into space so long that Ralph thought he was never going to answer. Finally the hamster said, "Take you for instance. Just where do you think you're going on that wheel?"

"No place, I guess," admitted Ralph. "I never thought much about it."

"See what I mean?" said Chum. "You run and you run and you're still in the same old cage."

Ralph felt suddenly guilty, as if he had done something wrong, but was not sure what it was. "But I like running on my wheel," he said, feeling that his answer was rather lame.

Chum did not bother to reply. He continued to sit, swinging, staring, thinking.

Ralph leaped to his wheel and began to run. His paws flew along the wires of the wheel, pushing it faster and faster until he looped the loop. He ran on and on until he began to tire. His paws touched the wires more and more slowly until Ralph coasted to a stop. Then he, too, sat staring and motionless. Where was he going? No place, that was where he was going. No place at all. With so many people feeding him, he was not even sure who owned him. Perhaps when the camp closed at the end of summer he would be turned out to the mercy of Catso and all those kittens. Drat Chum and

his talk about life, thought Ralph crossly. He
has spoiled all my fun.

Chum had still another habit disturbing to
Ralph. Whenever his owner approached him
with a bag of sunflower seeds, Chum suddenly
appeared to change from a grouch into an
agreeable pet. He climbed to the top of his
cage, accepted sunflower seeds one by one,
and stuffed them into his cheek pouches.

Feeding sunflower seeds to Chum became
a daily event in the craft shop. The older
campers and some of the counselors gathered
around Lana to watch her feed Chum, and as
she handed him the seeds they would count.
"Fourteen . . . fifteen. . . ." Ralph watched
while Chum's cheek pouches began to bulge.
"Twenty-two . . . twenty-three. . . ." Still
Chum's face stretched.

The old show-off, thought Ralph. "Twenty-
seven . . . twenty-eight. . . ." Chum had grown
so top-heavy that Ralph was sure he would
never make it to thirty.

"Thirty . . . thirty-one . . ." chanted the

campers. Chum was having such difficulty hanging on that Ralph scarcely could bear to watch. "Thirty-three. . . ." Those paws were slipping. "Thirty-four. . . ." Chum could no longer support his weight. He fell to the bottom of his cage with a thump that made Ralph cringe.

"Thirty-four!" shouted Lana, who enjoyed the attention her pet had received from older boys and girls. "That's Chum's record!"

"Maybe he'll hit thirty-five tomorrow," someone said, as the campers lost interest in the hamster and went off to their riding lessons or back to their craft work.

Chum got to his feet rather groggily and went to the storehouse corner of his cage where by placing his front paws behind his cheek pouches he pushed the seeds out of his mouth until they lay in a heap at his feet.

Ralph was disapproving of the whole performance. "That's quite an act," he remarked. "Doesn't it hurt when you fall to the bottom of the cage?"

"Sure it hurts," said Chum, as he pushed out the last sunflower seed. "But it's worth it."

"Just to show off?" asked Ralph.

"No, stupid," said Chum. "For the sunflower seeds. Sunflower seeds that I don't have to pick out from a lot of alfalfa pellets. I perform; she pays off in sunflower seeds. That's the way it goes."

"Yes, but you get hurt," said Ralph.

"I hate alfalfa pellets," answered Chum simply.

Ralph's turn came after lunch when the campers were in the dining hall singing a song that they obviously enjoyed, but that Ralph found frightening.

"Bill Grogan's goat was feeling fine,
    Ate three shirts right off the line."

Garf silently pushed open the screen door, and Ralph leaped from his wheel. Quickly Garf unlatched the door of the cage and extended a sunflower seed with his fingers. This

time he was not singing, but Ralph still did not
trust him. "Come on, fellow," coaxed Garf.
Ralph retreated to the corner of his cage behind his exercise wheel.

"Maybe next time," whispered Garf, and
hurriedly cleaned the cage and refilled the
water bottle while the campers sang on:

> "The whistle blew,
> The train drew nigh.
> Bill Grogan's goat was soon to die.
> He gave three groans of mortal pain,
> Coughed up the shirts and flagged the
> train."

When the song was finished, the house-
keeping for Ralph was completed, and Garf
had slipped quickly and silently out of the
craft shop without letting the screen door
slam or squeak. Ralph stood on his hind legs
holding the bars of his cage with his front paws
and wishing Garf were a different kind of boy.

Almost at once the screen door opened

again, and Aunt Jill with her arm around Garf's shoulders brought the boy back inside. "Sit down, Garf," she said, and sat on a bench beside one of the worktables. Scowling, the boy obeyed.

"What's the trouble, Garf?" asked Aunt Jill kindly.

What does she mean? Ralph wondered.

Garf stared at the floor.

"You know you have been breaking one of the camp rules," said Aunt Jill. "Campers are not supposed to come into the craft shop without permission unless I am here or one of the counselors."

So that is why he's always in a hurry, thought Ralph. He isn't supposed to be here. He not only likes bloodthirsty songs, he breaks rules.

Garf continued to stare at the floor.

"Is there anything we can do to help?" persisted the camp director.

"No," said Garf suddenly. "Because I'm going to run away, and nobody is going to stop me!"

Aunt Jill appeared to take this news calmly, but for some reason Ralph did not. He felt a shock of excitement. Don't do it, boy, he wanted to squeak. It won't get you anyplace. At the same time he realized that a boy who wanted to run away was sure to like motorcycles. Maybe he had misunderstood Garf. Maybe Garf liked speed and would know how to make a miniature motorcycle run.

"Is there someplace you especially want to go?" asked Aunt Jill.

"No," said Garf. "Just away."

Aunt Jill looked thoughtfully out the back window toward the barn and the riding ring before she turned to Garf and asked, "What do you want to do? What do you *really* want to do?"

Ralph gripped the bars of his cage and waited for the boy's answer. Catso's paw appeared through the hole in the screen door, but the human beings did not notice. Ralph watched and listened.

The hole in the screen had stretched another half inch.

Garf picked up a scrap of plastic left over from someone's lanyard and twisted it around his fingers. "I can tell you one thing," he burst out. "I don't want to braid any stupid lanyards! I've braided lanyards in Cub Scouts, I've braided lanyards at the YMCA, I've braided lanyards in the park during the summer, and I've braided lanyards in the after-school recreation program. Nobody needs more than one lanyard, and I'm fed up with lanyards!" After this outburst he sat staring at the floor, and when Aunt Jill remained silent, he went on. "And I want people to stop feeding my mouse. I caught him, and he's my mouse."

That's good, thought Ralph, because if he runs away he might take me, and then maybe I can escape and find my motorcycle again.

"I think that can be arranged," said Aunt Jill. "You've told me what you don't want to do and what you don't want other people to do. Now tell me what you want to do."

Ralph could tell from Garf's silence that this request was a difficult one. Aunt Jill seemed to have plenty of time to wait while he thought. Outside the craft shop some boys were gathering bamboo husks to float in the irrigation ditch. Ralph watched to see if they might uncover his crash helmet and motorcycle, but they did not go to the far side of the bamboo.

"Well ... uh," began Garf, and stopped.

Aunt Jill waited. So did Ralph, who noticed that Chum was also listening. Garf looked uncomfortable. Still Aunt Jill waited. Go on, say something, thought Ralph.

When Garf finally spoke he no longer sounded angry. "I guess ... I guess I just want to be alone *once* in a while," he said.

"You want to be alone," repeated Aunt Jill.

"Yes," said Garf. "At home I have to share my room with my big brother who gets the top bunk and keeps his weight-lifting stuff all over the floor. And every time I go to our room and shut the door, he comes in and starts playing those records I don't like. And after school and on Saturdays it's always Scouts or the Y or supervised recreation on the playground. My mom and dad say city kids have to be kept busy. And then they send me here."

"So they sent you to camp," said Aunt Jill, encouraging him to go on. "And you come into the craft shop to be alone."

"Yes," said Garf. "I don't like to sit around after meals with a bunch of kids singing *You Are My Sunshine*."

But you come in here and sing about the rabbit banging mice on the head, thought Ralph.

"I don't like singing with other people," said Garf, "because I can't carry a tune. I know I sing funny, and I don't like people turning around staring at me."

"Nobody cares whether you can carry a tune

or not," said Aunt Jill, "but if you don't want to sing, you don't have to. And we all need to be alone sometimes."

For the first time Garf looked at the camp director.

"And I know something that might help," Aunt Jill continued. "See that clump of bamboo over there? Any time you feel like being alone, you may go sit behind the bamboo as long as you wish."

Garf looked as if he wanted to believe her.

"Remember, Garf," said Aunt Jill, "it is possible to be alone in your thoughts even when there are others around." She rose from the bench where she and the boy had been sitting and found a piece of cardboard and a felt pen from the supply shelves. "Now about your mouse. You take this pen and make a sign saying this is your mouse and no one else is to feed it. I'll sign it to make it official, and we'll tack it up over his cage."

Garf did not say anything, but he took the cardboard and the pen and settled down at a table to work. He found a ruler and marked straight lines on the cardboard to guide his printing. He worked a long time, ignoring the lanyard braiders, mosaic makers, and insect collectors who came and went. A few people paused to see what he was printing, but no one disturbed him.

Ralph sat watching quietly as the sign progressed. Sometimes Garf paused to whisper rhymes to himself. "My, try, pry." "Pow, how, mow." "Read, lead, feed." Then he would go on with his work. He printed a few letters, stared at the ceiling, whispered to himself, and printed a few more letters. Near the end he held up his work, studied it, and added something more. When at last he had laid down his pen and stood up, Aunt Jill came over to look at his sign:

Pryvat! Keep Out!
This Mowse Is the Personul Property
of Garfield R. Jernigan
If you Fead Him You Will Drop Ded.
SIGNED. . . . .

Aunt Jill signed her name on the dotted line. "There!" she said. "That makes it an official Happy Acres Camp sign." She found two thumbtacks, and Garf tacked his sign above Ralph's cage.

For the first time Ralph saw Garf grin, and when the boy left the craft shop, he did not sit behind the bamboo as Ralph had expected. He stopped to watch some campers who were jumping and bouncing on the trampoline under the direction of a counselor.

Contented for the moment, Ralph made himself into a ball in the corner of his cage to enjoy a nap. He was not just any mouse. He was the personul mowse of Garfield R. Jernigan, a boy who wanted to run away, and the next time he was alone with his owner he would be brave and speak up no matter what dreadful song he sang.

6

A Thief
in the
Craft Shop

At first the sign over Ralph's cage was the cause of argument. "But Aunt Jill, how come Garf is the one who gets to feed the mouse?" the campers asked. "I want to feed the mouse, too." "Why can't I feed the mouse?" "It isn't fair. Nobody else has a mouse."

Aunt Jill always gave the same answer. "Garf gets to feed the mouse, because the mouse is his. He caught it in a butterfly net."

This policy inspired some of the campers to go mouse hunting—big-game hunting, they called it—with butterfly nets, but when no mice were caught, enthusiasm waned, and the campers gradually lost interest.

Catso followed someone into the craft shop whenever he could, and whenever he succeeded, Aunt Jill said, "Someone had better put that cat out."

Usually Lana was the one who picked up Catso and held him with his face over her shoulder as if he were a baby. "Poor baby," she crooned, patting Catso on the back as if she were burping an infant. Ralph found the smug look on Catso's face most annoying.

Garf was happy, but Ralph was not. The boy showed no signs of running away, and now that he abided by the rules, the two were never alone. The bars of Ralph's cage enclosed a very small area, and no matter how fast he ran on his wheel, he remained in the same place. He began to sit motionless for long periods of time while he thought more and more about the freedom he had enjoyed back at the Mountain View Inn. He missed those long corridors and his exciting expeditions in search of food. What he had once called crumb scrounging now seemed a test of courage. He even came to admit that he missed his little brothers and sisters and cousins. They were nuisances, but they were livelier than a grumpy hamster. Perhaps he wouldn't mind giving some of the little mice—boy mice, of course— short rides on his motorcycle after all.

Most of all Ralph missed that motorcycle.

He clutched the wires of his cage and, recalling the nights he had sped through the corridors of the old hotel while guests snored behind closed doors, tried to pretend they were the grips on his handlebars. *Pb-pb-b-b-b. Pb-pb-b-b-b.* It was no use. The wires remained what they were—the bars of a small prison, higher but not as long as an economy-sized Kleenex box.

Ralph grew listless. So great was his homesickness that choice tidbits from the dining hall tempted him less and less. He sometimes skipped meals, preferring instead to curl up in a corner under some shredded paper where he dozed, dreaming of dark nights, smooth floors, and speed.

"Cheer up," said Chum. "You'll get used to a cage."

Ralph did not answer. He wanted to be alone with his thoughts.

Garf, on the other hand, no longer wanted to be alone. He came into the craft shop to tend Ralph while other campers were present, and soon he became interested in the tools in the shop and finally went to work with some other boys building wooden boats to float in the irrigation ditch.

One long morning Ralph passed the time by watching a girl named Karen. Karen was one of the older campers, a girl twelve or thirteen years old with long blond hair, which, that morning, was wet. All the older girls washed their hair several times a week. Karen was making an old plastic bleach bottle into a piggy bank. She turned it on its side so the handle was on top, glued corks in place for legs, cut a slit under the handle, and painted eyes above the spout, which was now the piggy bank's snout. Ralph noticed that Karen paused from time to time to scratch her left arm.

Finally Karen set her paintbrush across the top of the paint jar and removed her wristwatch, which she laid on the shelf beside Ralph's cage. He could hear it tick. She scratched the spot where the watch had been, returned to her painting, and then stopped to scratch again.

"Karen, let me see your arm," said Aunt Jill, who was showing a boy how to lace together a wallet. "Why, it looks to me as if you have poison oak. You had better go see the nurse about it. And be careful not to scratch it."

"But Aunt Jill, it feels so *good* to scratch," said Karen, tossing back her hair.

"I know, but scratching only spreads the poison oak and makes it worse," said Aunt Jill. "Now run along and see the nurse. I'll wash out your paintbrush for you. It's almost time for the dinner bell."

When the bell rang for the noon meal and the craft shop was empty, Ralph felt his fur rise along his spine. Sure enough, just as he expected, there was the curious paw of Catso exploring the hole in the screen door. Then the pink nose appeared. Catso must have pushed hard, because the rusty screen gave way and the rest of his head appeared. Catso did not stop there. He pushed and wiggled until he got one shoulder and then the other through the hole. Then came Catso's front feet followed by the rest of the beast. Catso was in the craft shop! Where was Sam? Ralph scuttled to the far corner of his cage, where he turned his back to the world and tried to make himself invisible. He heard Catso land lightly on the worktable beneath his cage and knew that this time there was no one to snatch the cat and shove him out the door.

Ralph waited, but when nothing happened, he summoned the courage to peek over his shoulder. Catso was calmly washing himself and appeared not to notice. Ralph was not fooled for an instant. He knew Catso was aware of every move he made. Drat that cat, he thought bitterly, as his heart beat faster than the tick of the watch on the shelf beside his cage.

Catso licked his right paw over and over with great care and began to wash his right ear. That's right, thought Ralph. Take your time. He was worn out from bracing himself for the pounce that did not come. A real war of nerves, he thought, just what that cat wants. He's got me where he wants me, and he knows it.

Catso groomed his left paw, currying his fur neatly in the direction of his toes. He used his teeth to pull bits of dried mud from between his paw pads, and then began to scrub his left ear. Well, come *on*, thought Ralph. Get it over. You don't have to be so neat. He would just as soon be knocked off his shelf by a cat with dirty ears as a cat with clean ears.

Catso finished washing, looked at Ralph and glanced away. Ralph, who was familiar with that maneuver, thought, Here it comes! But this time Ralph was mistaken. Catso's attention had been caught by the leather strap of the wristwatch hanging over the edge of the shelf. He tapped it with a curious paw and watched it swing back and forth. Ralph's blood chilled as claws appeared from the exploring paw that batted the strap once more. Then the claws hooked the watch strap and dragged the watch down to the worktable. Why, that stupid cat actually thinks the watch band is a tail, thought Ralph in astonishment.

Catso sat very still listening to the watch tick. He batted it experimentally with his paw, but the watch lay as still as any terrified mouse. While Ralph watched in fascination, Catso picked up the watch in his mouth and, with the strap hanging down like a tail, leaped from the table to the floor where he dropped the watch, batted it about, picked it up again, and slipped out through his hole in the screen door.

Ralph ventured out of his corner and with shaking paws clung to the wires of his cage to

see what happened next. Catso played with the watch awhile on the bamboo leaves, but when the cook with a pan of scraps in hand opened the kitchen door, the greedy animal dropped the watch and ran off to be fed. The watch slid on a smooth bamboo husk until it came to rest, hidden from sight, under some leaves.

"Talk about close calls," said Chum.

"Stupid cat," said Ralph in a weak voice.

Ralph was dazed by the whole experience, but he noticed Garf leave the dining hall when the campers began to sing one of their favorite songs:

> "Up in the air, Junior Birdmen,
> Up in the air and upside down.
> Up in the air, Junior Birdmen,
> Keep your noses off the ground."

Come into the craft shop, Ralph pleaded silently.

True to his promise to Aunt Jill, the boy did

not enter the craft shop, but sat alone with his thoughts, twirling idly in a tire suspended from one of the trees, and singing to his private tune:

> "When you hear the doorbell ringing
> And see the badge of tin,
> You'll know the Junior Birdmen
> Have turned their boxtops in.
> B—I—R—D—M—E—N! *Yea!*"

Before long Karen, her left arm covered with white lotion, came running into the craft shop with two of her friends. "My watch!" she cried, sending Ralph scuttling into a corner. "It's gone."

"Somebody must have taken it," said one of her friends, an older girl who was wearing polished English riding boots.

"I'll bet it was that Garf Jernigan," said the second friend.

"I'll bet it was, too," said the girl in English riding boots.

"I saw him leave the dining hall early." She brushed dust from the toe of her boot. Girls who owned English riding boots were proud of them and shined them often.

Karen tried to be fair. "We don't *know* it was Garf, and we didn't *see* him come in here."

The girls crowded out through the screen door to meet Aunt Jill, who had paused on her way to the shop to talk to someone. "Aunt Jill! Aunt Jill!" they cried. "Karen's watch is gone!"

"Aunt Jill, we have a mystery!" cried Lana, who had tagged after the older girls in her dirty cowboy boots. She liked the dirt on her boots, which showed she was not a newcomer to camp.

Everyone wanted to hear about the missing watch. Campers crowded around Aunt Jill and the three girls. Through the open window Ralph could hear snatches of conversation. "Aunt Jill, I'm *sure* I left it on the shelf beside the mouse cage. I'm positive!" "—looked every-place—" "And I saw Garf—" "—and it was my birthday present—" "—search the lodges—"

"He sneaks out of the dining hall—" "—hasn't even been excused from the table—" "Now, girls—" (This was Aunt Jill.) "Well, I don't care. He acts funny—"

That cat really has fixed things now, thought Ralph, as the campers gathered on the benches and at the old school desks under the walnut trees. One of the counselors led the singing, and then Aunt Jill stepped up on the platform. "Campers, I have some unhappy news today," she began. "Karen's watch is missing from the craft shop, where she is sure she laid it on a shelf. It was not an expensive watch, but it was a birthday present to Karen, and she would like very much to have it back." Here Karen nodded her head vigorously, and Aunt Jill went on. "We are not going to search the lodges as someone suggested. We are going to let the person who took the watch return it, because it is the right thing to do."

A lot Catso cares about doing the right thing, thought Ralph. He heard Garf who was sitting on the last bench say angrily to the boy in front of him, "What are you looking at me for?"

Aunt Jill continued. "No one needs to know who took the watch. It can be returned to the shelf in the craft shop when no one is looking or to my desk in the office. We are not interested in who took the watch. We want it returned to Karen, because returning it is *the right thing to do.*"

After Aunt Jill's speech, the campers began to sing *You Are My Sunshine*. Garf slipped away from the rest of the campers and, as Aunt Jill had suggested, sat down by himself behind the clump of bamboo. This afternoon was the first time Ralph had seen him sit there.

"You make me happy—" sang the campers.

They haven't made Garf happy, thought Ralph, wishing that Garf were sitting on the other side of the bamboo near the craft-shop door where he might find the watch by accident.

"That boy is really in trouble," remarked Chum.

Ralph turned in surprise. "I thought you were asleep under your cedar shavings," he remarked.

"That's what I make *them* think," said Chum. "I didn't miss a thing."

"What is your opinion of the case?" asked Ralph, who knew the right words to use in such a situation from watching so many television programs in the lobby of the Mountain View Inn.

"I think that boy is in a tight spot," said Chum. "Everybody knows he used to come into the craft shop when no one was here, and they know he is still the first person to leave the dining hall, so naturally everyone thinks he took the watch. He obviously can't return the watch, because he doesn't know where it is, so of course everyone will think he is keeping it."

"That's the way I had it figured," agreed Ralph.

"And I can tell you one thing," continued Chum, "he's not going to come near the craft shop until that watch is found."

"But what about me?" squeaked Ralph in dismay, thinking of the sign above his cage. "Nobody else feeds me. I'll starve!"

"I'll try to toss you an alfalfa pellet once in a while," said Chum generously. "My aim isn't very good, but I should be able to get one into your cage now and then. Enough to keep you going."

Going where, wondered Ralph. No place. What was to become of him when the summer ended and all the campers went home? Would Garf take him away or would everyone forget him and leave him to starve? He did not want to spend the rest of his life in a cage, and he certainly did not want to be kept alive on a few cast-off alfalfa pellets only to starve at the end of the summer. There was just one answer. Ralph had to escape.

The campers finished a rousing chorus of *You Are My Sunshine*, when Ralph's sharp ears caught a sound that had him on his feet in an instant. *Pb-b-b-b. Pb-b-b-b.* It was the sound a boy uses to make a toy motorcycle go! It was made softly as if by a boy alone in his thoughts. Garf had found Ralph's motorcycle!

"Hey!" squeaked Ralph at the top of his small voice. "That's my motorcycle!"

Garf stopped pushing the motorcycle across the bamboo leaves just long enough to make Ralph think he might have heard. Then, to Ralph's disappointment, he put the motorcycle in the pocket of his jeans and went off toward his lodge for the rest period required of all the campers.

Ralph was so excited he left the bars of his cage and went for a run on his wheel. Garf spoke his language! He knew how to make the motorcycle go. There was hope after all. All Ralph had to do was explain to Garf—

As Ralph thought the matter over, his exercise wheel moved more and more slowly until it came to a stop and Ralph sat back on his haunches. His plan would not work. Until Garf was cleared of the theft of the watch, he was not going to risk coming into the craft shop. Ralph had to agree that Chum was right.

7

The
Escape

Ralph was desperate to escape. His food supply was running low, and as Chum had predicted Garf stayed away from the craft shop. Ralph ran around the sides of his cage hoping that there might be an opening, one overlooked space wide enough for a mouse to squeeze through. There was none, as he had known all along. He pushed on the door with all his strength, but he could not budge it. He ran on his wheel in hope that it might, just once take him someplace, but of course it did not. Ralph needed help.

"Hey, Chum," he called over to the hamster, who was noisily wearing down his teeth on the bars of his cage. "You're a stretchy fellow. See if you can stretch over here and pull this door open."

For once Chum obliged by putting his shoulder to the bars of his cage, stretching his foreleg as far as he could, and reaching with his paw. He barely managed to flick a wire of the side of Ralph's cage with a toenail.

"There must be some way we can get out of here," said Ralph. "There's got to be."

"Not for me," answered Chum. "I wouldn't leave if I could. I've lived in a cage all my life, and I'm too old to start scrounging. Besides, I rather enjoy trying to bite the hands that feed me."

"I would rather scrounge than starve," said Ralph. He still had a supply of food, but he pawed through some old sunflower-seed husks to make sure he had not missed any edible bits.

Over in the dining hall the campers, unaware that a mouse was soon to starve, sang with gusto:

> "The ants came marching two by two.
> Hurrah! Hurrah!
> The ants came marching two by two.
> Hurrah! Hurrah!
> The ants came marching two by two,
> And the little one stopped to tie his
>   shoe."

As his food supply dwindled further, Ralph felt nervous and guilty. His mother had taught him to store food. The sight of the campers' mosaics made of dried peas and beans was hard to bear. He felt he would no longer object to a little dried glue on his food. When Chum managed to toss an alfalfa pellet into his cage, he was humbly grateful.

Outside his cage the campers went about their activities unaware of the desperate mouse in the craft shop. Lana cradled Catso in her arms whenever she could catch him, and the smug look on that cat's face was unbearable to Ralph. Karen returned to paint her bleach-bottle piggy bank. Everyone who passed her worktable asked if her watch had been returned, and Karen, busy with her piggy bank, shook her head.

Occasionally Ralph's ears caught the familiar *Pb-b-b-b, Pb-b-b-b*, and he looked out to see Garf pushing his motorcycle across a bench or around the edge of the pingpong table as if he were lost in a dream of speed and danger. The sight of his precious motorcycle made Ralph even more frantic for freedom.

And then to add to his troubles, there was still Catso, who had been only temporarily amused by the wristwatch and who would sooner or later, Ralph was sure, return to the cage. Ralph felt thin, nervous, and run-down. His cage was untidy even by mouse standards of housekeeping. "I wish I knew how to stage a jailbreak," he confided to Chum.

"If there is anything I can do to help, let me know," said Chum, and cracked a sunflower seed he had earned that morning when he had stuffed his cheeks until he had fallen to the bottom of his cage.

Chum might toss me a sunflower seed instead of those alfalfa pellets, thought Ralph crossly.

At rest period Aunt Jill came into the craft shop to straighten supply shelves. Ralph watched as she sorted dried seeds, which looked delicious, as well as weeds and pinecones. As he watched, he saw a possibility of help. After all, Aunt Jill, unlike most women,

was kind to mice. Looking as small and as pitiful as possible, Ralph clung to the bars of his
cage.

In time, Aunt Jill noticed him. "Hello there,
little fellow," she said kindly.

Ralph made his whiskers quiver. "Let me
out of here," he said, quite sure the woman
could not understand.

Aunt Jill smiled when she heard the mouse
squeak and offered him a sunflower seed,
which he snatched and cracked so greedily
that he forgot to look pitiful.

"My, but you're a hungry little fellow," remarked Aunt Jill, but she did not offer him
another seed. Instead, when the camp awoke,
she called to Garf, who came to the door of
the craft shop, but did not enter.

"Your mouse is hungry," said Aunt Jill.

"Somebody else can feed him," said Garf.

"He's your personal mouse," reminded Aunt
Jill.

"I didn't take the old watch," said Garf. "I
don't want to come in there."

"I am sure you didn't take it," said Aunt Jill calmly, "but don't forget that you wanted to be the only one to feed your mouse. He is hungry and his cage needs to be cleaned."

Garf hesitated, but entered the craft shop, and while Ralph scrambled around looking for a way out, he slid the bottom from the cage, changed the cedar shavings, and replaced it. He detached the water bottle, filled it at the sink, and was fastening it to the cage when Aunt Jill went out, leaving the boy alone with the two animals.

Here at last was the moment Ralph had been waiting for. "Say, Garf—" he began, but the boy, not expecting the mouse to speak, appeared not to hear. Ralph was desperate. "Say Garf!" he said at the top of his mouse voice.

When Garf glanced at him, Ralph said as loud as he could, "Listen to me! You know that motorcycle you've been playing with? It's mine."

Garf stared at his mouse. "You're talking,"

he said in an astonished whisper. "I don't believe it. You're talking!"

Ralph had spoken and Garf answered. They
were both so excited they were speechless.
Finally Garf spoke again. "Go on. Say something more."

Ralph pulled himself together and remembered why speaking to Garf was urgent.
"*Pb-b-b-b*," he sputtered, to show Garf what
he meant. "That motorcycle. It's mine. *Pb-b-
b-b*. That's the noise I make to run it."

"You're joking!" Garf continued to stare at
Ralph as if he could not believe what was
happening.

"No, I'm not," said Ralph. "I hid it under
the bamboo leaves just before that cat pounced
on me. I hid my crash helmet, too."

"Your *crash* helmet!" Garf could not help
laughing, which, of course, hurt Ralph's feelings. The boy pulled the motorcycle out of his
pocket, studied it, and then studied Ralph.
"It's the right size," he admitted. "If it's yours,
where did you get it?"

"Back at the Mountain View Inn."

"The Mountain View Inn!" Garf was surprised. "What were you doing there?"

"It is my home," said Ralph with dignity. "A boy who was a guest there gave me the motorcycle."

"No kidding!" Garf almost believed Ralph.

"Let me out of here," pleaded Ralph. "I'll show you I can ride it."

Garf looked as if he were tempted, but he said almost regretfully, "No, you might run away, and I want to keep you."

"Aw, come on, Garf," coaxed Ralph.

"Nope," said Garf, "and I've got to get out of here. Aunt Jill just left to give me a chance to return that watch, and I don't have it. I don't have it, and I don't know where it is."

Ralph saw an opportunity for bargaining. "I do," he said. "I know where the watch is."

"Where?" asked Garf.

"Let me out, and I'll tell you," said Ralph.

"No," said Garf. "I'm going to take you home with me."

"Your mother won't like it," said Ralph. "She'll make you get rid of me." He knew by the look on Garf's face that he had struck a sensitive spot so he continued. "She will say I am messy, and she will say I—smell."

Garf looked uncomfortable.

"Let me out of here, and I'll show you where the watch is," persisted Ralph.

Garf looked as if he might be tempted. He thought awhile, and said, "My mother might let me keep a mouse. It wouldn't hurt to ask. And I don't want to know where the watch is. If anyone saw me trying to return it, they would say I stole it and I didn't."

Ralph's hopes dwindled. "I know you didn't steal it," he said, "because I know who did."

"Who?" Naturally Garf was curious to know the name of the real thief.

Ralph considered. Should he tell or should he not tell? He decided that telling might convince Garf that he was trying to help him. "Catso," he said. "Catso the cat took it."

Garf gave Ralph a look of disgust. "Now I

know you're lying," he said. "What would a cat do with a watch?"

Ralph was beginning to feel frantic. "Pretend it's a mouse. Play with it. Toss it around. You know how cats do."

Garf grinned. "For such a little fellow you sure have a big imagination."

"I'm *not* imagining it," said Ralph. "Catso took it. I saw him. Honest."

"Aw, you just don't like cats," said Garf, and started to leave.

Ralph sat miserably back on his haunches. "Well, even if you don't believe me, don't forget to feed me."

"Glad you reminded me," said Garf, and gave Ralph a generous supply of food before he left the craft shop. He paused by the bamboo where he had found the motorcycle, stirred the leaves with his foot, and uncovered the thistle-down-lined half of a pingpong ball, which he picked up and examined. He glanced back in Ralph's direction before he put the helmet in his pocket and went to his lodge.

In a few moments Aunt Jill returned, glanced at the shelf beside Ralph's cage, and frowned slightly as if she were puzzled about something. Ralph settled greedily at his food dish. I'll show that Garf, he thought, as he crammed seeds into his mouth with his paws. As soon as I get out of this cage I'll show him.

When Ralph's stomach was comfortably full, he took a long nap. By the time he awoke the craft shop was empty, the camp strangely quiet. A few chickens scratched under the walnut trees, and the kittens tumbled about trying to catch one another's tails. A horse whinnied in the pasture, but there was no one in sight. "Where is everybody?" Ralph asked Chum.

"They've all gone down to the river for a swim and a picnic supper," answered Chum. "Peaceful isn't it? I finally got some sleep in the daytime."

In the distance Sam barked and campers shouted and laughed. Ralph felt so stodgy from overeating that he went for a run on his wheel before he scuttled around the edges of his cage. His search was futile. Garf had replaced the bottom and fastened the door securely.

Suddenly the hair along Ralph's spine began to tingle. Catso! Ralph huddled in the corner of his cage and tried to make himself invisible. Catso squeezed through the hole in the screen and landed with a soft thud on the workbench beneath Ralph's cage. Ralph squeezed himself into a tighter ball. He felt as if the beat of his heart was as loud as the tick of the missing watch. Why couldn't Sam stay home and guard the camp the way he was supposed to? This time there was no watch to distract Catso. Catso stood with his front paws on Ralph's shelf and sniffed the cage. Then he sat down and calmly began to wash. First his right ear, then his left. The suspense was more than Ralph could bear. Catso stretched out his left hind leg and began to groom his left hind foot. He licked with long careful licks, combing his fur neatly toward his toes.

Suddenly Ralph had an inspiration. He was about to take a terrible chance, but with no one to protect him from a sneaky cat, he had nothing to lose. Anything was better than cringing in a corner waiting for that beast to wash and comb every hair on his body.

Ralph took charge. He left his corner, sprang on his wheel, and raced so fast he looped the loop. That activity caught Catso's attention all right! The cat sat there with his hind leg in the air looking surprised.

Ralph leaped from his wheel and faced Catso through his bars. The cat forgot about his grooming and, jumping to his feet, placed his front paws on the shelf and stared into Ralph's cage. Hiding his terror, Ralph stared back.

"If there's one thing I can't stand, it's a disrespectful mouse," said Catso, and with a swipe of his paw sent the cage flying.

Ralph was prepared. He hung onto the bars and braced himself. Water splashed and seeds flew. One corner of the cage struck the worktable, jarring the bottom loose, exactly as Ralph had planned. The cage bounced and landed on its side. Ralph sprang out through what had once been the bottom. This accident was his chance!

Catso pounced, but before his paws could land on Ralph he was thrown off his aim by a sudden hissing sound from above. Startled, he missed Ralph's tail by the width of a whisker. Ralph was startled too, but the unexpected noise did not prevent him from scrambling behind a jar of nails on the worktable.

When Ralph got up the courage to peek around the jar of nails, he saw Catso staring up at Chum's cage. He heard the hissing sound again and knew that it must be coming from Chum. Good old Chum! Ralph hadn't known that a hamster knew how to hiss.

When Catso recovered from his surprise he was after Ralph, who dashed from behind the nails as the jar was sent rolling across the table. Crash! It landed on the floor and broke, scattering nails across the craft shop. Ralph leaped

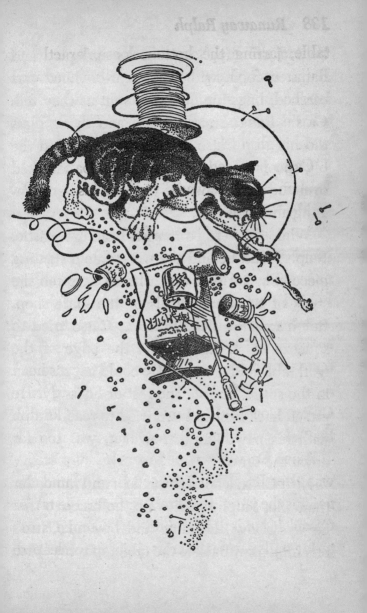

behind the supplies of beans and peas and hamster food with Catso after him. Jars crashed, bags tumbled and split as they fell. Crash! Bang! Smash! Noise and flying glass did not stop Catso. Ralph leaped behind the big spools of lanyard plastic. Catso knocked over the spools and the plastic unreeled, tangling about his feet.

While Catso freed himself from the plastic, Ralph found behind the worktable a slanting piece of wood that was a brace between the studs of the rough walls of the craft shop. Ralph ran down the brace as Catso tried to squeeze his head between the edge of the worktable and the wall. He could get his head in the space, but not the rest of his body. He pulled back his head and tried to reach Ralph with his paw. Ralph, however, was too far down the brace.

Next Catso leaped to the floor and ran under the table. Ralph scurried up the brace so that he was above the table and beyond Catso's reaching paw. Back to the tabletop went Catso and down the brace ran Ralph, once again beyond the stretch of those curved and groping claws.

Frantic with frustration, the cat sprang from the table while Ralph ran up the brace. Once more Catso reached and stretched and groped. Ralph's courage and confidence had returned. He advanced within half an inch of Catso's longest reach. Catso tried, but could stretch his foreleg no farther.

Ralph sat down, and said, "This could go on all day. You might as well give up. You know I'm too smart for you."

Catso, after one more effort to stretch farther, withdrew his paw, came out from under the table, and picked his way daintily and disdainfully through the jumble of seeds, nails, and plastic cord as if the mess was beneath his notice. He held his tail proudly erect, but he did not fool Ralph. That cat had been defeated.

Catso squeezed out the hole in the screen door. Ralph was safe! Safe and free. Now all he had to do was figure out how to get his motorcycle away from Garf, and he would be on his way back to the Mountain View Inn. In the meantime, he settled down to feast on all the seeds that Catso had spilled for him.

8

Ralph
Strikes
a Bargain

Lana was the one who discovered that Ralph was missing. The morning after Ralph's escape she came running ahead of Aunt Jill to the craft shop. She stopped short when she looked through the screen door and saw the litter of nails, seeds, and plastic strewn about the worktable and on the floor.

"Aunt Jill! Aunt Jill!" she shrieked, even though Aunt Jill was directly behind her.

143

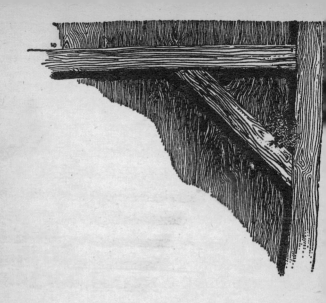

"Burglars have been here, and somebody stole Garf's mouse!"

Ralph crouched out of sight behind a fluff of dust in the angle where the brace joined the studding. He heard campers coming.

"Garf! Garf!" called Lana. "Your mouse is gone! Somebody stole your mouse!"

"Hey, look at the mess!" said Pete.

"The mouse cage is all bent," observed Garf. "A thief wouldn't have to bend the cage to open it."

"First a watch, now a mouse," said another camper.

"A thief in our midst!" cried Lana, eager for excitement and mystery.

"All right, boys and girls, let's pick up the nails and seeds and roll up the plastic." Aunt Jill's voice was calm. This crisis was not the first she had met at Happy Acres, nor would it be the last.

Then Ralph heard Garf's voice saying, "Look at that hole in the screen door. It's big enough for a cat to squeeze through."

Good thinking, Garf, said Ralph to himself. He had picked up this phrase from the many school teachers who had stayed at the Mountain View Inn while on their summer vacations.

"I'll bet Catso got my mouse," said Garf, adding sadly, "and he was such a good mouse, too."

Ralph could not help being pleased by this compliment, and a little sad, too. Of course, he was a good mouse. He had known that fact all

along, but hearing himself spoken of in the past made him feel that the world would have been a sadder place without him.

"Garf, you're a good detective," said Aunt Jill. "Catso must be the guilty one."

"Aunt Jill, you don't think Catso—*ate* the mouse, do you?" Lana was awed by the enormity of such a crime.

"I hope not, for Garf's sake," said Aunt Jill.

What about *my* sake? thought Ralph indignantly.

"We'd better look around," said Aunt Jill. "Perhaps the mouse is hiding someplace."

Instantly a mouse hunt was organized. Butterfly nets were seized, jars and boxes moved, craft materials lifted.

"Here, mousie, mousie," called Lana. "Here mousie, mousie."

As if I would come running, thought Ralph, huddled behind a dusty cobweb in the dark shadows.

"I guess he's gone," said Garf at last. "The first and probably the last mouse I'll ever have."

"Garf, I'm putting you in charge of repairing the hole," said Aunt Jill. "Get a piece of screen and some wire from Uncle Steve, and we'll make sure Catso won't come in here again. We wouldn't want him to annoy Chum."

At that point the fur along Ralph's spine began to tingle.

"There's Catso now!" cried Lana. Ralph felt the slam of the screen door jar the building as Lana ran out. "Bad cat, Catso! Bad cat!" he heard her shout. The scolding did Ralph's heart good.

Later that morning after his riding lesson, Garf returned with a piece of screen and some wire to repair the hole. His work was frequently interrupted as campers left the craft shop and drifted off to other activities. When Aunt Jill left, Ralph came down from his hiding place in a series of leaps. Through the screen door he watched Garf sitting on the step weaving the wire patch to the screen with a piece of thin wire, before he said, "Say, Garf, about my motorcycle—"

Startled, Garf looked up from his work. "You're alive!" His obvious pleasure was most gratifying to Ralph. "I thought Catso got you."

"How come you believed Catso got me, when you wouldn't believe Catso stole the watch?" demanded Ralph. "I can run and jump, you know, and a watch can't."

"It just isn't logical for a cat to steal a watch," Garf insisted.

"If I show you where the watch is, will you believe me?" asked Ralph.

With a look of interest Garf sat back on his

heels. However, he said, "I don't want to have anything to do with that watch. I don't want to be seen near it, or people will start saying I took it again. Most everyone's forgotten about it, and I want to keep it that way."

"You don't have to go near it," said Ralph. "Just watch me." Flattening himself, he squeezed under the screen door, jumped down the steps, and ran out into the bamboo leaves. Suddenly, all bamboo leaves looked alike. Which leaf was hiding the watch? Ralph did not know. He looked under one leaf, and then the next. He heard Garf mutter, "Huh!" and return to his work. Over by one of the lodges Lana shouted, "Bad cat! Bad cat!"

Ralph pushed some leaves aside and crawled under others. Where was that watch anyway? There was no telling how many leaves had fallen since Catso had dropped the watch. Ralph crawled deeper and deeper into the leaves and was finally rewarded by, the touch of metal against his paw.

Next Ralph grasped the buckle on the

leather strap and tugged. The watch was heavier than he had expected, but it slid across the smooth inside surface of the leaf. Ralph waded up through the leaves, pulling with all his strength, and at last emerged, dragging the watch behind him. "See!" he said. "I told you I knew where it was!"

"Well, what do you know?" Garf sat down on the step to the craft shop. "You really did. How did the watch get there?"

"I *told* you," said Ralph impatiently. "Catso picked it up in his mouth, carried it out here, batted it around awhile, and finally dropped it where it slid under a leaf."

"You know, I believe you're telling the truth," said Garf with wonder in his voice.

"Of course, I'm telling the truth." Ralph was indignant.

"But what good does it do me?" asked Garf. "You know I can't return it. And if I said Catso stole it, people would laugh."

This moment was the one Ralph had been waiting for. First he pulled some bamboo leaves over the watch to hide it before he faced Garf. "All right, let's talk business," he said. "I return the watch and clear your name; you give me back my motorcycle."

From the trampoline Ralph heard Lana say as she bounced, "Bad—dog—Sam! You're supposed—to be a—watch—dog!" She stopped bouncing and began to scold Sam. "You're a watchdog. Why didn't you watch what Catso was doing? Why did you let Catso get that poor little mouse?"

Garf thought awhile before he said, "Why do you want the motorcycle? The ground is pretty uneven around here."

"Why do you want it?" countered Ralph. "You're too big to ride it. It is mouse-sized, not boy-sized."

"I want it because I like to think about motorcycles," said Garf. "I push it back and forth and think about riding a motorcycle when I grow up."

"I want it to ride," said Ralph. "Now. Back to the Mountain View Inn. I want to go home."

"The Mountain View Inn!" Garf was incredulous. "That's over a mile away. You'd never make it."

Ralph recalled the long and thrilling downhill ride. He remembered how he had thought at the time that he would never be able to go back up the mountain road. "Maybe you're right," he admitted.

"Of course, you wouldn't," said Garf. He pulled the motorcycle out of his pocket and ran a finger over the front tire. "For one thing your tires would never stand the trip. They're wearing smooth. There is still a lot of mileage left in them if you ride on floors, but they won't hold up on a highway."

"Oh." Ralph had not considered the possibility of his tires wearing out.

"And another thing," said Garf. "You'd probably get laryngitis from making a motorcycle noise before you were halfway there."

Ralph was utterly dejected. "I suppose you're right."

"Bad—Sam! Bad—Sam!" scolded Lana from the trampoline.

Ralph ducked under a leaf while some campers walked past. "What am I going to do?" he asked pitifully, as he emerged. "I can't stay here with the cats. I'm a hotel mouse. I'm not used to living on weed seeds out in the cold. When winter comes I'll probably die—if the cats don't get me first. I've got to try to make it back to the hotel."

"You should have thought about things like that before you ran away," chided Garf.

"I should, but I didn't," said Ralph coldly. "You don't have to sound like a grown-up."

"Sorry," apologized Garf. The dinner bell rang, and campers began to run toward the dining hall. Catso, avoiding Lana with a haunted look on his furry face, darted from one hiding place to the next, on his way to the kitchen door. Poor old Sam, so conscientious and anxious to please, padded dejectedly across the grass with his tail drooping. He had failed in his duty.

Ralph did not have much time. "Do we have an agreement or don't we?" he demanded of the boy.

"I have a better idea," said Garf. "I'll take you back to the hotel myself when my family comes to get me. They'll be spending the night there before they come to pick me up the day after tomorrow. The camp doesn't serve us lunch on the day we leave, so I know we'll stop at the Inn for lunch before we start for home. It's the only place around here. I could easily take you along in my pocket."

This offer was more than Ralph had hoped for. "But the motorcycle," he persisted. "If I return the watch, will you give it back?" Ralph felt he would rather perish at Happy Acres Camp than return to the hotel without his motorcycle.

"How will you return it?" Garf was curious. "You couldn't get it up on the shelf in the craft shop or up on a desk in the office."

"I didn't say where I would return it," answered Ralph. "I said I would return it. I'll leave it somewhere where Karen is sure to find it."

Garf thought this plan over. "But people might think I left it there."

Ralph had an answer. "Not if I leave it someplace where the boys can't go."

"You mean the girls' bathroom?" asked Garf, visibly impressed by Ralph's idea.

"Maybe," said Ralph carelessly. "Or Karen's lodge. Or the girls' dressing room by the swimming pool. You better make up your mind or you'll be late for lunch."

"It's a deal!" said Garf suddenly. "You return the watch by tomorrow, and I'll give you back your motorcycle. The next day I'll take you to the Inn. But remember, no watch, no motorcycle."

"It's a deal," agreed Ralph, "and you might throw in a peanut-butter-and-jelly sandwich for my dinner."

"Would you care to shake on it?" asked Garf.

Ralph extended his paw, which Garf took gently between his thumb and forefinger. They shook. "I'll meet you by the bamboo tomorrow morning after breakfast," said Garf, and he ran off toward the dining hall. "If you're not there, I'll come back later."

I hope I'll be there, thought Ralph, who knew that a night of peril lay ahead of him. A peanut-butter-and-jelly sandwich would help to give him strength and courage.

Over in the dining hall the campers began to sing:

"You can't get to Heaven on roller skates
'Cause you'll roll right past those pearly
gates.
You can't get to Heaven with a nickel in
your jeans
'Cause the Lord don't allow no slot
machines."

9
A
Dangerous
Plan

I'm a failure, Ralph told himself, as the bird chorus announced the dawn and a rooster crowed down by the barn. I'm a miserable rotten failure.

Ralph had returned to his perch in the bamboo after a night spent hurrying, scurrying, and worrying. Every building at Happy Acres Camp was built on ungnawable mouseproof concrete. Every screen door was above a cliff-like concrete step. The watch still lay hidden in the bamboo leaves, Garf would soon learn that his name was not to be cleared after all, and Ralph would not get his motorcycle back. Drat, he swore to himself. Drat, drat, drat! He felt especially bad, because Garf actually had left a quarter of a peanut-butter-and-jelly sandwich at the foot of the bamboo for his supper the night before.

Ralph was about to climb down the bamboo to hide from Garf when the alarm clock rang, and the bugler stumbled out to rouse the sleeping camp. Campers washed their faces at washbasins outside their lodges, and then, before they went to breakfast, the girls carried their sleeping bags out to air. Some draped their unzipped bags on fences. Others, including Karen, spread theirs on the grass in the sun in the girls' area.

Why, here's my chance after all, thought Ralph in wonder, as a plan, simple but dangerous, sprang into his mind.

After noticing that Catso was sitting expectantly by the kitchen door waiting to be fed, Ralph leaped to the ground and found the watch under the bamboo leaves. Seizing it by the buckle on the leather strap, he began the labor of dragging the watch toward Karen's sleeping bag.

The watch was heavier than Ralph had remembered. He pulled and strained and managed to tug it across the gritty path to the craft shop and into the shelter of the grass. The watch slid more easily through the grass, and Ralph soon learned to choose the smoothest way, avoiding clods of dirt and prickly weeds.

The campers finished breakfast and came bursting out of the dining hall. Ralph toiled on, pulling the watch toward Karen's sleeping bag a fraction of an inch at a time, knowing that Garf must be searching for him by the bamboo. Ralph began a long hard detour around a fallen walnut and hoped that sometime Garf would at least know he had tried even if he might not succeed.

Suddenly the fur along Ralph's spine began

to prickle, and he froze in his tracks. Catso! The hunter's eyes of the cat had caught the movement of the grass. Ralph crouched motionless beside the watch.

Catso slunk close to the ground, moving so quietly he seemed to flow through the grass. Only the tip of his tail twitched. Ralph knew that trying to run was useless. Running would only make the hunt more interesting for Catso and prolong the misery for Ralph. Catso stopped and waggled his hindquarters experimentally, as if he were trying to find the most efficient position for pouncing.

Where was Lana? Ralph's life passed before his eyes—his family mouse nest back at the Mountain View Inn, his mother and Uncle Lester and all his brothers and sisters and cousins, the boy who had given him the motorcycle that had changed his life, the cage in the craft shop, Chum, Garf—

Catso crouched even lower and waggled his hindquarters once more in preparation for the pounce.

Ralph's eyes were distracted from Catso by Sam, who trotted purposefully across the grass. If one doesn't get me, the other will, thought Ralph, as he tried to shrink even smaller beside the watch. Surely a dog would not want to crunch a watch between his teeth.

Sam growled deep in his throat. Distracted, Catso stopped waggling and glared at Sam.

"Get me in trouble, will you?" growled Sam to the cat.

Catso stood up, arched his back, and appeared to double in size. "See here, Sam," he hissed. "I'm supposed to exterminate pesky mice."

"Not this one," growled Sam, advancing. "He belongs here, and you got me in trouble by letting him escape."

"Is that so?" Catso hissed back, as he swiped at Sam's nose with an evil clawed paw. "What about me? I'm unjustly accused of eating him."

"And what are you up to now?" demanded Sam, and with that question he snapped at

Catso, who turned his back and with his tail proudly erect stalked off toward the craft shop, before he suddenly remembered he had not washed lately.

While Catso sat grooming his toes, Sam eyed Ralph with interest. "You're a busy little fellow," he remarked, not unkindly. "First a motorcycle. Now a wristwatch." He thought a moment before he said, "Say, where did you get that watch? You didn't happen to steal it, did you? No. You couldn't. You're too little."

"That's right. I'm too little," agreed Ralph. "But Catso stole it, and I'm trying to return it to its rightful owner." He told Sam the whole story explaining why Garf could not return the watch.

Sam glanced at Catso and growled, but Catso merely paused in washing his left hind foot to look disdainfully at Sam, who then said to Ralph, "You're pretty little to be pulling that watch over this rough ground. Maybe I can help you out. Here, let me take it for you."

Ralph trembled to see that great snout coming close. He crept away from the watch and stared fascinated as Sam delicately picked up the leather strap in his teeth and trotted over to Karen's sleeping bag, where he dropped the watch on the flannel lining.

Ralph crept closer. "Thank you, Sam," he said, genuinely grateful to the big dog.

"It was all in line of duty," said Sam. "Still, one thing bothers me. Boys don't come into the girls' area, but couldn't a boy throw a watch over here? A boy could stand on the other side of the fence and toss a watch onto a sleeping bag. I'm not sure Garf's name will be cleared when Karen finds the watch."

"I never thought of that," admitted Ralph, "but give me a little time and I can take care of it." He scurried over to the watch and began to gnaw a hole in the fabric of the sleeping bag. Garf might be able to throw a watch, but he couldn't gnaw a hole. Sam settled himself with his nose on his paws to guard Ralph.

Ralph used his sharp teeth so efficiently that he soon had a hole in the dry and tasteless lining. He waded into the Dacron stuffing, dragging the watch behind him.

"You all right in there?" asked Sam.

"Of course, I'm all right," answered Ralph, shoving the Dacron aside to make room for the watch. The Dacron was softer than the most finely shredded Kleenex. It was softer than nylon stockings or pillow feathers or any other soft thing Ralph had experienced at the Inn.

"Then I'd better be on my way," said Sam. "I still have the barn to inspect."

Ralph popped his head out of the hole in the sleeping bag. "Thanks a lot, Sam," he said. "You saved my life. I really mean it." The watchband still protruded from the hole so Ralph crawled back inside and tugged some more until he was sure it was safely out of sight. There. When Karen climbed into her sleeping bag that night she was sure to feel a lump, investigate, and discover her missing watch in a place where Garf could not have hidden it.

The Dacron was deliciously soft, and Ralph

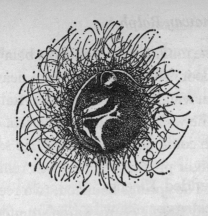

was tired after a sleepless night. I've got to get out of here before rest time, he told himself, but part of him answered, Go on take a short nap, only a minute or two. Rest time is a long way off, and you need some sleep. The Dacron was soft and cozy, the sounds of the camp were muffled, and Ralph was tired. . . .

The next thing Ralph knew, the sleeping bag was moving. He heard the swishing sound of a long zipper being closed and felt himself being lifted. Then a screen door slammed, the sleeping bag was set down, and a pair of hands smoothed it.

Drat! thought Ralph, now I've done it! He

heard the muffled sound of boots being thrown on the floor. The cot beneath him heaved, and a sudden weight seemed to flatten Ralph, even though he was cushioned by Dacron.

Ralph could not help himself. He squeaked. The weight pressing on him was removed instantly. The springs bounced, two feet hit the floor, and Ralph heard Karen's muffled voice say, "That's funny. I'm sure I heard a squeak."

"It's your springs, silly," said another girl.

"No," said Karen. "It was more like a mouse, and it was right under me."

"Quiet, girls. It's rest time," said the counselor.

I better get out of here, thought Ralph, crawling out of his Dacron nest and in between the two layers of flannel lining. As he started toward what he hoped was the open end, he heard the swishing sound of the zipper. The top of the sleeping bag was thrown back, and Ralph was exposed for all to see.

"E-e-ek!" squealed Karen. "It *is* a mouse! And he isn't even squashed!"

Ralph leaped to the floor and was aware of a double row of girls staring at him from their bunks. He darted toward an overturned riding boot, realized that he would be trapped inside, and darted the other way without knowing where he was going.

Now all the girls were squealing. "Catch him!" "Don't let him get away!" "Isn't he darling?"

"He isn't darling in my sleeping bag!" said Karen.

Sock-clad feet hit the floor. "Get a washbasin!" someone yelled. "Catch him under a washbasin."

"Girls!" cried the counselor.

Ralph darted this way and that. No matter which way he ran he met feet. He was frantic. He knew he had to find a way to escape before someone clapped something over him. The screen door creaked, so he knew someone had run outside for a basin.

"A hat!" someone shouted. "Where's a hat?"

In his panic Ralph ran up and over a foot

in a white sock. Its owner screamed. Sam, alerted by the scream, began to bark.

A straw cowboy hat plopped down on the concrete floor, making a dark dome over Ralph. The daylight that shone between the straws seemed like starlight to a mouse.

"Look!" shrieked Karen. "A hole in my sleeping bag! He chewed a big hole right in my sleeping bag!"

Sam, frantic to protect the girls, scrabbled his paws against the screen door.

"It's only me," squeaked Ralph, but no one could hear him.

Ralph was alert, waiting for someone to lift the hat so that he could make a dash, if not for a knothole, at least for the shelter of a bunk.

"There's something in the hole in my sleeping bag," cried Karen. "My watch. Look! It's my missing watch!" Feet went padding to Karen's bunk.

The screen door opened. One set of dog footsteps and two sets of human footsteps entered, those of the girl who had gone for the washbasin and those of someone else. "Girls, what is going on in here?" asked Aunt Jill. "This is supposed to be rest time."

Ralph could hear Sam snuffling around in circles with his nose to the floor.

The girls all tried to speak at once, but Karen managed to tell about the finding of the watch. "So Garf couldn't have taken it," said another girl.

"And we have the mouse in person right here under that hat," said another.

Sam's nose came to a halt at the hat brim.

"Hey, Sam. It's only me," squeaked Ralph in alarm. He was relieved to have Sam sit and begin to pant. Ralph pressed his eye to a crack in the straw and saw Sam's long pink tongue hanging out.

"But what I don't understand," said Karen, "is how the watch got inside the hole. A mouse couldn't put it there."

You'll never know, thought Ralph in grim amusement.

"Aunt Jill, what shall we do with the

mouse?" Ralph heard one of the girls ask. "We're going to scoop him up in this wash-basin."

Not if I can help it, thought Ralph.

"Why don't we give him to Garf?" suggested Aunt Jill. "I'm sure he misses his mouse, and I know his feelings were hurt because some people thought he had taken the watch."

"Good idea!" agreed Karen.

Well, thought Ralph, that takes care of a lot of things. When the brim of the hat was lifted and the rim of the plastic washbasin scraped against the floor, Ralph hopped into the basin and, with hat still held over him, felt himself being lifted. Then the hat was raised a few inches on one side of the basin, and Ralph saw a row of eyes staring at him. Ralph could not help trembling, even though he was sure he had nothing to fear.

"He's so *little!*" said one of the girls, marveling.

"Aunt Jill, he looks an awful lot like Garf's mouse," said Karen. "You don't suppose—"

"One mouse looks pretty much like another," said Aunt Jill briskly. "Now girls, back to your bunks. I'll take the mouse to Garf." Darkness fell on Ralph as she replaced the hat over the basin.

Ralph felt himself being carried out of the girls' lodge and past the craft shop, where he could hear Chum gnawing at the bars of his cage. Poor old Chum. He heard the door of Garf's lodge being opened. "Garf," whispered Aunt Jill. "Wake up. Wake up! I have something for you."

"Huh?" said Garf sleepily. Waking a sleeping boy on a hot summer afternoon is not easy.

"I have a mouse for you," said Aunt Jill.

"A mouse!" Ralph could tell Garf was wide awake now. "Let me see."

Ralph sat quietly in the basin while the hat was cautiously lifted. He could see the other boys and their counselor sprawled in sleep on their bunks, and on a ledge over Garf's lower bunk he saw his crash helmet. "Karen found him in a hole in her sleeping bag," Aunt Jill explained. "And it was the strangest thing. She found her missing watch inside the hole." Ralph saw that Aunt Jill was studying him thoughtfully.

"No kidding!" exclaimed Garf, forgetting to keep his voice down.

"Yes," whispered Aunt Jill, "and the girls thought you might like to have the mouse."

"I sure would!" whispered Garf.

"I think we can bend the cage back into shape," said Aunt Jill.

"Can't I keep him here in the basin?" asked Garf.

"He might escape," said Aunt Jill, "but he's your mouse." She smiled and slipped quietly out of the lodge.

"You did it!" whispered Garf.

"Sure I did it," said Ralph, "but do I have to sit here in this basin?"

"Of course not," answered Garf, holding out his hand.

Ralph leaped into Garf's palm, and Garf gently moved his hand down close to his pocket, and there, as he hoped, was his motorcycle. In the warm and cozy darkness he ran his paws over the handlebars, the plastic seat, the wheels, the exhaust pipe. The motorcycle was intact, and it was his once more. He had earned it.

Ralph popped back out of the pocket. "You aren't going to make me go back into that cage, are you?" he asked.

"Not if you promise not to run away. I'm taking you back to the Inn tomorrow. Remember?"

"You haven't forgotten your promise about the motorcycle, have you?" asked Ralph just to be sure.

"Nope," answered Garf.

"I won't run away," promised Ralph. "But there's one more thing. Before you leave camp, do you suppose you could give Chum a piece of wood to gnaw, so he won't have to gnaw his cage to keep his teeth worn down?"

"Why, sure," whispered Garf. "Right after rest time."

That need taken care of made Ralph feel better about Chum alone in the craft shop. He was about to climb back into the pocket when Garf whispered, "Do me a favor, will you? Let me see you ride the motorcycle before everybody wakes up."

"Sure!" Ralph was happy to agree to this request.

Gently Garf lifted Ralph and the motorcycle to the floor. Then he handed down the crash helmet, which Ralph set on his head and secured by snapping the rubber band under his chin. Expertly he grasped the handle grips, threw his leg over the plastic seat, and taking care to keep his tail out of the spokes inhaled.

Pb-pb-b-b-b. Ralph took off across the concrete floor while Garf leaned over the edge of his bunk to watch. Ralph bent low over his handlebars and increased his speed. *Pb-pb-b-b-b.* Filled with the joy and excitement of speed, he rode in a figure eight around Garf's cowboy boots, which were lying on the floor. Garf's counselor moved in his sleep, and

Ralph shot out of sight under Garf's bunk until the counselor lay still. He rode until he was breathless, and then he coasted to a stop in front of Garf, where he sat panting with his crash helmet pushed back on his head.

"Boy!" whispered Garf. "Was that ever great!"

Ralph silently agreed.

"I sure wish I could do that." Garf picked up Ralph and the motorcycle and put them gently in his pocket.

After all the excitement of the morning Ralph was ready for a nap, but first he popped his head out of Garf's pocket. "Thanks, friend," he said. "And by the way, don't roll over on me during rest time."

"Don't worry," whispered Garf. "I'll get you back to the Inn in one piece. And your motorcycle, too."

About the Author

Beverly Cleary was born in a small town in Oregon, where she lived until she reached school age. At that time her family moved to Portland, where she went to grammar and high school. After graduating from the University of California at Berkeley, she entered the School of Librarianship at the University of Washington in Seattle, specializing in library work with children. In 1939 she became Children's Librarian in Yakima, Washington.

In 1940 she married Clarence T. Cleary and they moved to Oakland, California. During World War II Mrs. Cleary was Post Librarian at the Oakland Army Hospital. The Clearys now live in Carmel, California. They are the parents of twins, a boy and girl.